A
MIGHTY
WALL

For Miss Jules and our son, Sean Michael.

JOHN FOLEY

A MIGHTY WALL

flux™
Woodbury, Minnesota

First Edition
First Printing, 2009

Book design by Steffani Sawyer
Cover design by Ellen Dahl
Cover photograph © 2008 Corbis/PunchStock

Flux, an imprint of Llewellyn Publications

Library of Congress Cataloging-in-Publication Data

Foley, John, 1960–
  A mighty wall / John Foley.
      p. cm.
  Summary: Seventeen-year-old Jordan, a skilled, self-confident rock climber, plans to turn his favorite sport into a lifelong career until an ascent near the small town of Vantage, Washington, turns deadly.
  ISBN 978-0-7387-1448-6
  [1. Rock climbing—Fiction. 2. Coming of age—Fiction. 3. Washington (State)—Fiction] I. Title.
  PZ7.F729Mi 2009
  [Fic]—dc22

Flux
Llewellyn Publications
A Division of Llewellyn Worldwide, Ltd.
2143 Wooddale Drive, Dept. 978-0-7387-1448-6
Woodbury, MN 55125-2989, U.S.A.
www.fluxnow.com

Printed in the United States of America

Also by John Foley

Tundra Teacher
Hoops of Steel
Running With the Wind

Author's Note and Acknowledgments

The descriptions of mountains and crags in *A Mighty Wall* are based mostly on first-hand observation, although some liberties have been taken for dramatic purposes. Zenny's account of the Everett Massacre and Pete's ruminations on Martin Luther are historically accurate.

While I'm a hiker rather than a climber—given the option, I go around cliffs rather than up them—I do admire those daring athletes who test themselves against sheer walls and big mountains. Many climbers helped me during the course of researching this novel.

I am deeply indebted to my friend and fellow writer Fern Chandonnet, who introduced me to mountaineering in the Chugach Range outside Anchorage, Alaska. Fern is a wonderful raconteur, and his incisive wit and great spirit made him an ideal companion in the mountains.

The Everett branch of the Mountaineers provided me with much information through their Alpine Scrambling class, and leaders Neal Breshears, Rick Proctor, and Lyle Harvey were especially generous with their knowledge.

I'm also grateful to Eric Smith, a climber and teacher at Cascade High School in Everett, who let me pick his brain about climbing psychology and various crags in Washington. Math teacher Marilyn Mallory was kind enough to let me observe her class, as well.

Melissa Arnot and Alaina Robertson of Rainier Mountaineering, Inc. provided excellent instruction in alpine mountaineering. Olivia Cussen of Northwest Mountain School (and RMI) gave me a rock climbing lesson in Leavenworth and patiently answered my questions afterward. Climbers Chad Kellogg and Tim Matsui graciously granted an impromptu interview at the base of Index Town Walls. And the folks at Vertical World in Everett showed me what indoor climbing is all about.

Finally, I'm grateful to my wife Julie for reading the manuscript and providing a valuable first edit; the team at Flux—Brian Farrey, Sandy Sullivan, Courtney Kish, and Andrew Karre; and my agent Alison Picard.

ONE

No act of kindness, however small,
is ever wasted.

—Aesop

Whic I was six, my parents rented a camper and
took a long June weekend trip to Mount Erie in
Anacortes. I have a vague memory of the trip, but last
year, when my world went wild, it seemed important to
know exactly what had happened. Mom filled in the gaps
for me.

On a Friday afternoon they parked at a little campground behind a general store on the banks of Lake Erie.

After a cookout we all walked up the road a quarter mile or so—there was hardly any traffic—and then turned onto a steep trail bordered by huckleberry. I sort of remembered that Mom and Dad were more affectionate than usual, kissing and holding hands and hugging. Didn't mean anything to me at the time; just an impression.

We came to a bench and rested while looking down at the lake, the horse pastures, the slice of Puget Sound beyond a ridge, and the Olympic Mountains in the hazy distance. That was all fine, but when I turned around and looked up at the rock cliffs above the trail, my world changed.

"Looking for mountain goats?" Mom asked. "It's too steep for them."

I was absolutely awestruck by those towering walls of granite. Something about them seemed both forbidding and inviting.

That night in the camper, I dreamed about cliffs. I woke early and dressed quietly while listening to the soft snoring of my parents in the front berth. I lit out before dawn.

Despite the darkness, I found the trail easily enough. At the bench I turned toward the cliffs and bushwhacked my way to the base, getting cut by the alder sometimes. I have a vivid memory of looking up and seeing a full moon in the clear sky above the rocks.

And I started climbing.

The holds were good, even though I didn't know anything about holds or three-point protection or that stuff. But climbing was natural to me. Before I knew it I was fifty feet up, then one hundred. I found a nice ledge and rested while the rising sun colored the lake a soft yellow.

Above the ledge I couldn't find any good grips. So I decided to go down. I'd barely started when I realized it would be much harder to climb down than up. I couldn't locate the holds with my feet. I don't recall being afraid so much as frustrated by the new problem. I was still trying to figure it out an hour later, when I saw Mom and Dad running along the trail below.

"Mom," I yelled. "I'm up here! Up here!"

They looked around, and Dad spotted me. "There he is!" he yelled, pointing at me. "Oh, Jesus, there he is!"

"Oh!" Mom yelled, and her hands flew to her mouth.

"You okay, Jordo?" Dad asked.

"Yeah, but I can't figure out how to get down."

"Stay there!" they both yelled at the same time, extending their hands toward me. Mom burst into tears and Dad held her while she cried.

When she stopped crying, she started climbing. Dad got ahold of her foot before she was out of range. "Angie, honey, wait! We need to think about this. Wait!" She tried to kick him away for a second, then slowly nodded her head and hopped down.

They talked for a while. Sometimes they looked up at me, sometimes they shouted at each other. Eventually they seemed to reach an agreement.

"Jordo, you okay for a little while?" Dad asked.

"Yeah," I said. "My butt hurts a little, but I'm okay."

"Don't stand up!" they both yelled.

I nodded. This was something new—my parents yelling a lot. They yelled a little bit, every now and then, but never this much.

I saw movement on the trail below. Mom and Dad heard the voices about the same time I did. Two guys, one tall and one short, both thin and young, rounded the switchback a few seconds later. Mom and Dad jogged over to them, pointed at me, and they all started talking. Mom said, "Rappel? He can't rappel."

"I'll be controlling him from the top, you from the bottom. It won't be rappelling, really, just lowering him," the tall guy said.

"No, there's a low angle. He'd be banging against the rocks all the way down."

More talk. Finally, the tall guy started to get a rope and other stuff ready, with help from his friend.

"You still okay?" Mom asked.

"Yup," I said. "But I'm getting hungry." Mom laughed and Dad smiled. There was a crazy edge to Mom's laugh, and she started crying again.

The tall guy disappeared at the base of the cliff. A few minutes later I heard breathing and movement below me, then saw his face up close. He wore glasses.

"Hi Jordan," he said. "How you doing?"

"I'm okay."

"Good. I'm Tom, and I'm going to help you down."

"Okay."

"You need to do exactly what I say."

"All right."

"First, I want you to move about four inches to your right. Just a little bit, got it?"

I nodded and moved, and heard Mom gasp.

"Good job, Jordan. Now I'm going to sit down next to you."

He stepped and turned and was sitting next to me a second later. Our legs touched.

"That's a pretty good climb you did," he said. "Always remember it's harder to climb down, in a lot of places."

"Yeah, it is."

He worked for a while with a rope and metal things that he carried. "Got the bolt in, but I don't like it enough to rappel," he said to the three faces below. "I'll down-climb with him."

He told me we were going to play slow motion. "Move like you're under water, Jordan. Real slow. I want you to get this harness on. Just do as I say."

I nodded, and a few minutes later I had the harness on. Sort of. It was way too big, even with the straps adjusted as tight as they would go.

"Gravity will keep you in the harness, Jordan ... Shit, you probably don't know what gravity is ... Uh, sorry I said shit."

"It's okay, Dad 'n Mom say that sometimes, then say sorry, too."

He smiled. "This is the tricky, part, pal. I'm going to clip your harness to my harness. I'll need your help. Let's think about this … Okay, I'm going to put a carabiner on your harness. Let me show you how these things work."

His finger pushed against one side of the carabiner it clicked open. He did it a few times. Then he put it through the loop on the front of his harness and screwed it shut. "See that? Do you think you can do that?"

"Yeah."

"Good. Watch a couple more times. Now, you're going to hook the 'biner through the loop in your harness and the back of my harness … Think you can do that?"

"Yup."

"All right. I could do it, but I'd be off balance and fumbling around. It will be safer if you do it." He reached around his back and showed me where to clip onto his harness. "I'll check it when you're done. So Jordan, I'm going to turn a little to the left, and you do the same. Here's the carabiner. Go for it."

"Okay." We turned and I clipped it onto my loop and his harness belt. I noticed that he held my leg with his right hand. Then he reached back, tested everything, and spun the carabiner gate shut. "Good job, Jordan, you're a natural. So now I'm going to climb down. I need you to relax and hold on to my waist. Don't touch my arms, shoulders, or neck, okay?"

"Okay, let's go."

He snorted a little laugh. "On belay?"

"Belay on," his friend called.

"Climbing!"

Then Tom quickly turned toward the cliff, and I was hanging in space. I heard Mom gasp again. He stopped when he had his hands on the ledge. "How you doing, Jordan?"

"Good."

"Thataboy. Stay cool."

He climbed down a few more feet. The rope on our right went up as we went down. I saw some metal things the rope went through sometimes. He moved slowly, and sometimes stopped to talk to his partner below.

"I know there's a hold around here somewhere, Jordan, but I'm having trouble finding it. Stay cool, buddy."

He felt all around with his fingers. I remembered that from that angle, I could look through the right lens of his glasses and see distorted gray rock.

"Found a little one," he said, loud enough that I knew he was talking to his friend. "Gonna go for it. You ready?"

"Got you, Tom."

We dropped suddenly—he'd taken a big step, but we didn't fall. I saw his right arm extended over to a small rock, the muscles in his forearm knotted with tension. He was breathing harder. The moment passed, and he descended the next twenty feet smoothly.

Hands were grabbing me and Mom was crying. They

got me out of the harness, and then she started shaking me. "Don't you ever do that again! Ever! You scared us, Jordan! First we thought you drowned in the lake. Then your father remembered how you looked at the cliff, and we came up here. Don't you EVER do that again!" Then she hugged me. Then she started shaking me and yelling again.

Tom and his friend were watching silently. Over Mom's shoulder I saw Tom sort of smiling, and he winked at me. Dad shook their hands and Mom hugged them both. Dad tried to give them money, insisted, but they refused and said they were glad to help.

Dad came over and hugged me when Mom was done shaking me. Quietly, he said, "I don't want you to climb anything when you're alone, Jordo."

"I NEVER want you climbing ANYTHING again," Mom said. And she gave Dad the evil eye.

"Okay," I said, mostly because they were so freaked out.

. . .

"Never" lasted about three days. Then they caught me in a tree in the backyard. That's when they decided to bag it and, after a lot of discussion, Dad took me to a local climbing gym in Everett.

I've been a climber ever since. I know it's dangerous and all, and I've had some close calls, but there's nothing

I'd rather do than head up a fine crag … Well, maybe one other thing. Climbing Girls are hot.

Juana just hit me. She's my girlfriend, and when I told her I was going to write about everything that happened, she told me she'd edit the story. She's planning to be an English teacher, and she's already a good poet, so she knows all about that stuff. I don't mind her editing, except when she's looking over my shoulder and hitting me when I write a questionable line. Of course, Juana is a climbing girl herself, so for all she knows I might have been writing about her, and her alone.

This time she gave me a light slap. Guess she doesn't buy it. Oh well.

TWO

Myths. Meyer says we build our own myths.
We live in the flatlands and the myths are our
mountains, so we build them to change the contours
of our lives, to make them more interesting.

—John D. MacDonald

My dad died a couple of years after my first climb. I was still pretty young, so I really don't remember the whole thing. I don't miss him as much as I would have if I'd been older and spent more time with him. I do feel sad when I think about all the stuff we could have done together, and sometimes at night I hear Mom crying in her room, and I know she's crying about him.

He was on a business trip in Mexico and died of natural causes. A few times I tried to get Mom to be more specific, but she gets angry and emotional and just can't talk about it. Asking about how he died is like torturing her, so I haven't asked in years.

Still, I wonder. He was in his early thirties and in great shape, so how did he die of natural causes? I figure it was like those basketball players and track stars you hear about who suddenly collapse because of a congenital heart problem, which made me wonder about MY heart, but the doctor who gave me a physical last year said I was completely healthy and very fit, so no worries.

Actually, I take that back. I do have a couple of worries about my bod. Well, not worries, more like peculiarities that bug me. The big one is my satellite dishes, as I jokingly call my ears. They stick way out of the side of my head and are extra large.

Mom keeps saying I'll "grow into them," like my head will grow sideways or my hair will become three inches thick. When I was twelve I slept for a while with a fat book on the side of my head, alternating each night, trying to push my ears flat. Mom caught me one night and said it was a good way to go deaf. We had one of the infamous mother-son chats. It was better than the sex chat—but not much.

My other peculiarity is one I mostly like. I have very long arms for my size. I'm a shade under five-seven, so it might not sound like much, but my wing span is almost six feet. This comes in very handy when I'm climbing, and that's the part I like. The part I'm not crazy about it that my arms naturally swing too much when I walk. Other kids have noticed, and since sixth grade the nickname for me has been Monkey Boy.

My friends know I don't like that and call me Jordan or Jordo. I never really had any enemies until recently, but kids who don't especially like me or just enjoy being jerky still call me Monkey Boy. I've tried to shrug it off and joke about it and all that, even though I really hate that nickname. Who wants to be compared to a lower primate?

Because I'm skinny and vertically challenged, I was hazed a bit as a freshman at Mountain View, the big high school I go to in Everett. Got tossed in a garbage can, stuff like that. Then I made friends with a couple of dudes who pretty much assured me a bully-free life, at least while I'm in high school.

I met A.J. Stevens at the climbing gym before our freshman year. I was already working at the gym and taught him in the belay class, and we hit it off. And he brought in Casey Ragurski after football season that year.

Actually, I'd already met Casey because we were in the same English class. I couldn't believe he was a freshman. He was six-three and two-thirty then, already shaving and looking like a big college guy. I was five-two as a freshman and barely a hundred pounds.

So one day in English I'm walking back to my seat after turning in an essay, and my feet leave the ground.

Casey had come up behind me, grabbed me under my pits, and lifted me up over his head. He carried me to my seat and plopped me down.

"You were moving too slow," he joked, "and looked like you could use a lift."

Everyone cracked up, including the teacher. I was a little embarrassed, but I could see it was kinda funny and that he didn't do it to be mean. Ever since then, if he spots me in the hall or the lunchroom or just walking somewhere, he'll try to sneak up behind me and give me a lift. Of course, big as he is, I have to be really into the tunes on my iPod for him to sneak up on me.

A.J. was instantly one of the most popular guys at school, and Casey the biggest, so, like I said, I didn't get hazed after I began hanging out with them.

A.J.'s popularity made it tough being his friend sometimes. The world around him was pretty crowded, and often at school he'd be literally surrounded by people trying to talk to him—mostly girls. There were three reasons for this: He's a superjock, good looking, and just a nice, sociable guy.

His athletic ability became obvious when he was a freshman on the football team. A.J.'s not that tall either—just five-nine—and he wasn't much taller than me when we were freshman. But he was the fastest guy on the team, and I mean the whole team, varsity and everybody. Still, the coaches made him play on the freshman team the first game, then moved him up to varsity after he ran for a couple hundred yards. Casey knocked out like five guys in that game, so the coaches moved him up, too.

As for A.J.'s looks, they're a little unusual but girls go crazy for him. He's half white, a quarter black, and a quarter Native American. The way it breaks down, his father is half black and half white, his mom half Lummi and half white. All this left A.J. with a tan complexion, straight dark hair, wide dark eyes, and high cheekbones. He's also friendly and happy and smiling all the time. With everything he has going for him, why wouldn't he be?

At a basketball game sophomore year, I overheard a couple of girls talking about A.J. He leads cheers in the stands at games, sitting on top of Casey's shoulders and acting like an orchestra conductor. So anyway, this girl says to her friend, "You should just go up to A.J. and tell him he's the most gorgeous thing you've ever seen and see what happens."

There have been three or four serious girl fights over A.J. at school every year. Principal Denny called A.J. into his office one time and, only half joking, told him that if another cat fight broke out, A.J. would be suspended along with the combatants. The girls all figure he'll just fall for them and not look at other girls, but A.J. doesn't like to do one thing at a time.

"I tell them I'm a player, up front," A.J. told me at the gym one time. "They don't believe me. Or they think they can change me. But I'm a free agent and like lots of girls."

I've become friends with some of A.J.'s rejects. A couple of them even told me I was cute. Not handsome—cute, like a brown-haired puppy dog. The most I got was a little make-out action. Girls don't go wild over cute. Must be my damn ears.

. . .

Anyway, life at school is pretty good because I'm in A.J.'s circle. I also like Mountain View overall. It's located a little south of downtown, on the highest ridge in the area, and has a great view of the Cascades, including Mount Baker to the north and Rainier to the south.

Watching the sun rise over the peaks on clear mornings almost makes up for the ungodly early starting time—seven thirty. I read a news story online about how teens need more sleep than adults, and that some school districts around the country have pushed back starting times to eight thirty or even nine. I'd second the motion.

Other than that and a few assholes, Mountain View is cool. It looks almost like a small college, with grassy common areas between buildings. The only problem with that is it makes skipping class a lot easier. The school cop, Officer Michaels, and another security guard named Brockman roam the campus in golf carts—it's kind of funny to see them chasing kids in those things—but there are dozens of good hiding places if you really want to skip.

Mountain View takes a lot of crap from other schools because of its mascot—a Sasquatch. Yeah, we are Sasquatch, hear us roar. There's a school down in southern Washington that has a fierce-looking potato for a mascot, and they're called the Spudders. That's definitely worse, and they probably take more grief than us. We're right with them at the bottom, though.

About twenty years ago a talented student sculptor named Matt Clarkson created a statue of a Sasquatch and it stands to this day at the center of the school, on a concrete common area between the math building, cafeteria, and administration building. Our Sasquatch is about eight feet tall and holds a big stick in his right hand.

Clarkson did a great job with the sculpture, but he didn't depict anything between the big guy's legs. It's obviously a guy, because it has no boobs and a heavy beard—even Sasquatch women probably don't have THAT much facial hair. So, no rack and no buddy down below, what's up with that? We figured the artist probably caved to pressure from the administration at the time.

Like all true artists, though, Clarkson found a way to fulfill his vision. If you stand twenty to thirty yards away from the Sasquatch, on the north side at an oblique rear angle, the stick he holds parallel to the ground looks like a huge hard-on.

Some students on the school paper, the *Free Sasquatch*, managed to slip a picture of our mascot—from that point of view—into the paper my freshman year. So many copies were made that the administration has never been able to obliterate the image from campus, despite serious efforts.

■ ■ ■

Until this year, I never had any serious problems at Mountain View. Well, I take that back. I did get in a little trouble freshman year. It started with the Stay in School program. Every two weeks we'd meet with an advisor—a teacher on staff—who would show us stats on the money high school graduates make versus non-grads, motivational videos, stuff like that. Bottom line, Mountain View wanted to increase its graduation rate.

So one day we were supposed to list careers of interest, and I wrote *professional climber* and *second-story man*. Well, the teacher went berserk. My counselor went berserk. My Mom went berserk. I was in big trouble, and only got out of it by telling them I was joking.

I wasn't.

The way I figure it, I could travel around and climb great walls during the warm months. And during the winter, I'd head down to Miami Beach and secure funds from greedy old farts in high rises. I'm not sure where I got the idea, maybe a movie or something, but I started thinking about it in seventh grade. And the more I thought about it, the more I liked it.

So I'd go in late at night, grab the jewelry and cash lying around, and be out in a few minutes. Probably clear five grand on a good night. I'd do the Robin Hood thing, giving some to the poor to keep my karma cool, and put the rest in the bank.

Only problem with the plan is my recurring nightmare. Most people would probably be afraid of falling, but I scouted out high rises around Seattle and the holds look good, so that doesn't worry me at all. No, in my nightmare I'm scaling a high-end condo on Miami Beach. Below me Biscayne Bay is shining in the moonlight. I'm climbing strong and soon reach the twenty-first floor, where I locate an open balcony door. Then I tiptoe inside and leave the door open enough so I can make a hasty exit. I'm looking around for money and stuff when I hear, "Move and I'll blow you away."

I hold my breath and turn. She steps in front of me, holding a gun. About eighty years old with a prune face, droopy breasts, and more spots than a Dalmatian. "Help out an old woman or you're history, Sonny," she says, and takes off her nightgown.

I wake up in a cold sweat, and tell myself that it was just a dream. Hope so, anyway. I don't know if I could handle an occupational hazard like that.

THREE

Be bold—and mighty forces
will come to your aid.

—Basil King

G o for it, Lisa, you got it!"
"Mom, get me a chalk ball."
"On belay?"
"Cross, cross, sidepull!"

This was the sound of business, on a Friday evening in early May, at You So Mighty, the climbing gym where I work. I was behind the counter when Pete walked in.

"Get your goddamn hand out of the till, Jordo, you can't put anything over on me."

"Naw, I only steal from the rich in high places."

"Correct me if I'm wrong, but you have yet to begin your career as a second-story man."

"True, Pete. Maybe I should start taking a few bucks from you, just for practice."

He smiled at me. Pierre "Pete" Reinard is the owner of You So Mighty. He's pushing fifty, but he's in fantastic shape. He lifts weights a few times a week at Gorilla Gym down the block, free-climbs nearly every wall at the gym a couple of times a week to test the holds, does a little top-roping at the crags, and bikes and hikes with his girl-friends.

Actually, he only has one girlfriend at a time. Just seems like they overlap because, to borrow a basketball phrase, Pete has a high turnover rate. He likes younger women and they seem to like him, too, at least for a couple of months.

I was a little surprised to find out Pete's a stud because he's not exactly an ace in the looks department. His nose is too long and his mouth too wide. He's bald on top and his gray-brown hair is long on the sides and pulled into a ponytail in back. He covers some of his baldness with a beret. He has a bunch of them, all different colors, and the joke around the gym is that he even wears a beret in the sack.

In his face, he pretty much looks his age, but from

the neck down he's a much younger dude. Even under his pile jacket you can tell he has a buff upper body, and he walks around the gym like he's got springs in his shoes.

Pete lived in France as a kid and is fluent, and sometimes I'll see him reading a French novel behind the counter. He's always reading something and has a huge vocabulary, even though he dropped out of high school and joined the navy. Mom mentioned that Pete cusses like he's still in the navy. She hardly ever cusses and most of the teachers at Mountain View would probably bite their tongues off if they uttered an obscenity, so the contrast is funny to me.

A few minutes after accusing me of stealing from him, he said, "Goddamn, Jordo, you're getting fucking taller every time I see you. I think you'll end up five-four when you top out."

He's six-two and likes to tease me about my height, knowing I really don't mind. When I started working at the gym as a freshman, I told Pete that my mom was going to take me down to Disney World over the holidays, and he said he hoped they'd let me on the rides. That was the first time I called him an asshole, and he cracked up. He likes when you give it back to him.

After I got to know Pete, I asked him where he got the name for the gym. "Well, twenty-odd years ago I was down in California with some climbing buddies," he said, "driving east from Oakland, and we stopped for a bite. This guy walks in and asks—with a straight fucking face mind you—if anyone knows the way to You So Mighty. I thought he was joking despite the dull aspect of his visage, but no, there wasn't a trace of irony. He was entirely serious! He saw Yosemite on the map and came up with that pronunciation. We started laughing our asses off and this dullard stared at us like *we* were the idiots!"

There was a bit more to the story. "A couple weeks later," Pete added, "a lovely but grammar-challenged lass from Argentina used that exact phrase as a post-coital compliment. I took it as a sign."

I nodded. It used to take me a bit longer to unravel some of Pete's sentences. Hanging around him has improved my vocabulary, I know that. I still go home and look up some of the words he uses. Like the other day, when a city councilman dropped by with some "literature." Pete said, "It's not remotely literature, there's nothing literary about it. You want to garner some votes, you should be honest and say it's a pamphlet full of proletarian wanker bullshit."

Pete can rub some folks the wrong way. He's just himself, and doesn't care at all what people think of him.

He opened the gym in downtown Everett about eight years ago, in an old three-story warehouse. I joined as a climber right away—the fifty-foot walls were much higher than those at the gym I'd climbed at before. Pete is always tinkering, but the basic layout hasn't changed much. Up front he sells climbing gear—shoes, harnesses, ice axes, belay devices, stuff like that. In the center of the gym area are some low open lockers for gear, chairs for relaxing, and mats for stretching. Around that are twenty-one walls ranging from 5.0 to 5.15.

The ratings for roped climbs start at 5.0. By the way, the rating system—which is a little subjective but fairly accurate—is called the Yosemite Decimal System. Yosemite is considered the best rock climbing area in the United States, and one of the best in the world. I plan to head down there someday, maybe after graduation. Mom made it clear she would never give me permission to go as long as I'm under her roof, which I understand. Climbing big walls can be dangerous.

Anyway, on that evening I had a belay class to teach, with five people signed up. I'd been teaching it for almost two years and had it down. I like helping people learn the right way, so they're safe.

The first few times I taught the class I was nervous, especially if I was teaching adults. Now I don't care who is in the class. Well, maybe I'd get nervous with a class full of supermodels, but that's about it.

We met at the front counter. Three guys in their early twenties, a girl about my age, and an older woman who looked sort of familiar. I said hello and told them to grab a harness and follow me into the gym, and then we'd do the introductions.

"I'm Jordan Woods," I began. "This is a belay class, which is required if you want to climb at You So Mighty."

The woman was smiling at me. "The tables have turned," she said. "You don't recognize me, do you?"

And then I suddenly did recognize her. Took me a minute because she was older in the face and thinner in the body. "Hey, Mrs. Hampton, how you doing?"

"Great, but I now go by Ms. Seachord, my maiden name. And you can call me Marie."

"Uh, okay," I said. Calling your fourth grade teacher by her first name is tough, but I gave it a shot.

The girl was named Juana, the guys Rick, Trajan, and Mason. I showed them how to get into the harness, which can be tricky the first few times. "The most important thing to remember about the harness is to double back the waist strap. That ensures it won't come loose."

I went over belay devices, carabiners, and the figure-eight knot. You have to tie a single figure eight, then put the rope through the leg and waist straps of the harness, then retrace the figure-eight knot, which, if done right, will be secure as Fort Knox.

"A little trick," I noted, "is to retrace in the tight part of the knot, rather than in the big empty area that looks inviting."

The girl smirked. I noticed that she'd tied her knot in about five seconds, perfectly. She was lean, and had that climber look that's hard to explain—something daring in the eyes and graceful in the movements.

"You've climbed before, Juana?" I asked her. I'm getting pretty good at remembering people's names in my classes.

"Yeah, I was in a gym in Eugene," she said. "I was hoping that would qualify me to skip this class, but the guy on the phone said no, it was required."

"Yeah, it is. We just don't know how experienced you are, and it's a liability thing."

She nodded. "My dad says everything is a liability thing these days."

She was cool and very cute, with pouty lips, short honey-colored hair, and big amber eyes. I would've liked to talk to her some more. Had to focus on the class, though.

I went over the belay motion and commands and had them practice over and over. Takes awhile to get them down. Basically, you're feeding the rope through the belay device as your partner climbs. You have to be alert because if your partner falls, you need to pull down hard on the rope in front of the device. That's called a brake, and immediately stops the fall. The physics of friction.

The commands I taught them are mostly common sense. "On belay?" means "duh, are you ready to belay me?" "Climbing" is self-explanatory, too. The command "take" means "take my weight on the rope."

"And 'Falling!'" I told the class, "is one we hope to avoid saying." That got the usual chuckle.

Mostly I'm serious, though. Like I emphasize that the belayer's brake hand never, ever leaves the rope. "You don't know when your partner might fall," I said. "You have his or her life in your hands, literally. So always be ready."

The class ended with them belaying each other. Marie and Juana paired off, and I ended up working with Trajan, the odd guy. Odd as in mathematical, not strange. He was a bit unsure of himself at first, but seemed confident by the end of class. Pete stepped in then to introduce himself and welcome everyone to the gym.

"Pete," I said, "this is Marie. She was my fourth grade teacher."

"Hello, Marie," he said, shaking hands. "Let me ask you, how much responsibility do you assume for Jordan's illiteracy and general failure as a scholar and citizen?"

She was stunned for a second, then laughed. "Well, as I recall, he was a very bright and well-behaved child." She winked at me. "And I'm proud that he's turned out to be a fine young man—and a good teacher. Thank you for the belay lesson, Jordan."

"You're welcome, Mrs ... Marie."

Pete and Marie chatted a bit more. The guys left with waves and smiles. Juana was bouldering—which means climbing on a low wall that doesn't require a rope. I walked over.

"Nice tattoo," I said.

"Thanks, I got it last year. Freaked out my folks, but they said I could get a tattoo for my sixteenth birthday."

It was on her shoulder blade and showed a silhouette

of a woman in classic climbing position, one leg bent, one extended, one hand on an invisible rock, one reaching. Below the silhouette it said CLIMBERGIRL.

She hopped down and turned toward me. "You're a good teacher, Jordan. I expected to be bored but it was okay."

"Hey, thanks. So where do you go to school?"

"I start at Mountain View next week."

"That's where I go."

"Do you like it?"

"Yeah, it's okay. Most of the teachers are pretty nice."

"My parents keep telling me all the great things they've heard about the school, and they found this gym and signed me up. They know I'm pissed about moving and not finishing the school year in Eugene, so they're working hard to make it as painless as possible."

"Well, hope you like Mountain View. I know you'll like the gym."

"You're biased, but I gotta admit, it's better than the gym at home. Bigger walls and some higher ratings. What's with the quotes at the top?"

"Oh, Pete's a literary guy, so he puts up quotes he likes about climbing and other stuff. They're small so you can't read them unless you top out on the route."

"That's tight. I like literature. He's pretty funny, too."

"Yeah, I started climbing here when I was nine, so I've known him a long time. We're friends, even though he's an old guy." I said the last part louder than I had to. Pete was still talking to Marie, and he turned and laughed.

"Damned ingrate! Give you a job to get your urchin ass off the streets, and that's the thanks I get. Put the shop to bed, Jordo. I'm going for a cup of coffee with Marie."

"Okay, Gramps."

Juana was laughing. She had perfect teeth and her eyes crinkled shut. I stared a little too long, and she noticed. Damn, I wish I was as smooth with girls as A.J.

"I have to do some paperwork," I said, "so you could boulder about ten more minutes if you want."

"Nah, I should get going—it's a school night," she said sarcastically. "Maybe I'll see you at Rocky Mountain High or whatever it's called."

"Yeah, and let me know if you want me to belay you sometime. I mean, you know, we could climb together."

Shit! "Belay" sounds way too much like "lay." I thought I'd blown it completely, but she was still smiling. Maybe she didn't notice, or didn't mind.

Maybe I still had a shot.

FOUR

*Climb the mountains and get their good
tidings. Nature's peace will flow into you as
sunshine flows into trees. The winds will blow
their own freshness into you and the storms
their energy, while cares will drop off like
autumn leaves.*

—John Muir

I was dreaming about climbing Nutcracker in Yosemite,
stretching for a hold in the runout crux, when I heard
a shout. The sound shocked me and I fell...

Into consciousness. Mom was yelling, "Get up, Jordan, time to hike!"

She has way too much energy in the morning.

"Come on, get ready," she shouted from the doorway.
"We're climbing Mount Si today. Did you forget?"

I yawned. "Naw, I remember. What time is it?"

"Six o'clock."

I stared at her through bleary eyes. "It's Saturday. You're getting me up at six o'clock on a Saturday?"

"Yup, a lovely soft Saturday morning. Lots of folks will be heading out of town, so I want to get going early, beat the traffic. Quit whining and start moving."

I was tempted to say something smart, about how she could start without me and I'd sleep a couple more hours and still beat her to the summit. Didn't want to get grounded, though—she says I whine too much, and she gets mad about it sometimes. "You better take me to Starbucks," I mumbled as I swung my feet to the floor. Mom smiled.

"You got it. I want to get out of here in a half hour, so don't lollygag."

I nodded and headed toward the bathroom. Mom had this goal to climb Mount Rainier in June, and I'd gotten dragged into the deal. It all started at Thanksgiving. We drove down to spend the day with relatives in Kirkland. While I was putting up with my Uncle Jim and cousins Jimmy Jr. and Sarah—they're all kind of arrogant and annoying—Mom was in the kitchen with Aunt Mary. They were preparing the feast and I guess Aunt Mary said something about Mom taking up a lot more room in the kitchen than she used to. Mom was fuming all the way home.

Weird how things work sometimes, because the put-down inspired her. She had let herself go a bit and was about twenty pounds overweight, and she wasn't doing much to stay in shape besides walking a couple of miles through the neighborhood now and then.

Well, that night she ran. And the next day she joined the gym. She was sore for a couple of weeks, but she didn't miss a single workout because of that or anything else. I mean, she was *driven* to be fit again, and she got there pretty quick. She'd lost about twelve pounds, and I'm sure she would've dropped more except she was turning it into muscle, which, as my gym teacher Mr. Hall likes to point out, is heavier than fat and looks better, too.

To stay motivated—she couldn't keep being pissed off at Aunt Mary—Mom set the Rainier goal sometime in December and signed us both up with Tahoma Peak Guides. She gave me the confirmation e-mail as a Christmas present, and I thought it was a cool plan. She kept running and lifting weights to prepare, and in April she started hiking up the Mount Si trail in North Bend every Saturday, rain or shine. She naturally wanted to drag me along, do a mother-son bonding thing, and that wasn't so cool. Especially this early in the morning.

The hike itself is okay, I guess. I was always awake and feeling better about it by the time we got to the trailhead. Some Saturdays I wished I could take a pass on hiking and do some crags with A.J. instead, but when I mentioned that to Mom, she looked a little hurt. So we negotiated a deal that called for me to go top-roping on

Little Si with A.J. every other Saturday, after we were all done with Mount Si. Little Si is a nothing hike, but the north side has a great wall. Mom would meet a friend from Issaquah for lunch on those days and do some shopping, then come back and pick us up.

I took a quick shower and got dressed, and loaded up my fanny pack. Mom takes a full pack with all this extra crap—first aide kit, rain gear, parka, emergency shelter ... I tease her that she forgot the kitchen sink. Anyway, she worries that I'm not prepared if things go wrong on the mountain.

"People die on smaller mountains, too," she said. I argued that if a storm moved in I could always run down the mountain, which would get me back to the car fast and keep me warm on the way. She shook her head. "What if you broke your leg? You'd die of hypothermia."

"With a couple hundred other people on the trail? No way, Mom." She's much too cautious sometimes, and is always worried about me when I go out to the crags. She wishes I'd just be a gym climber, and a mountain hiker like her.

She argued some more that morning, and we compromised again. I agreed to a rain slicker, hat, gloves, water, and food in my little pack. For some reason my legs don't get cold unless it's like below zero out, so I just wore shorts.

We stopped at a Starbucks on the way out of Everett, then headed south on I-5 and 405, hooked up to I-90 and headed west to the hills through a light rain. The coffee helped and I was feeling better by the time we arrived at the trailhead. Lots of other early birds were there, too.

I took a leak in the foul-smelling outhouse. Mom went ahead, knowing I'd catch her, and I did before she reached the second switchback. The Mount Si trail is four miles one way. Took Mom two and a half hours to reach the summit area on her first climb in early April. This time she was hoping to break two hours.

The lower trail was getting better every week. On our first hike, the mud slowed us down and left us looking like little kids who'd had a fight in a puddle. I guessed there still might be some mud near the top, from the snowmelt.

We climbed steadily in the misty rain, not talking much. Mom insisted we stop when we reached the benches two miles up. She gulped water from one of the liter bottles she carried. I had a bladder pack with water and just took a sip now and then, but I did eat a granola bar.

"You ready?" I asked after a couple of minutes.

"Jordan, you can't rush through life all the time," she said. "Stop and smell the roses every now and then."

"There are no roses here."

"Don't be so literal. Smell the fir trees, look at the meadow goldenrod, listen to the bluebirds. You know what I mean."

Mom's Miss Nature. The last few hikes, she'd pointed out birds and flowers and things, the fire damage to the

Doug firs in this flat section—I think it was to stall for more rest. She seemed pretty strong today, though, so I guessed she wasn't using the wonders of nature as an excuse to catch her breath.

A guy sitting on another bench chuckled at our conversation. He said, "You have the right attitude. I mean, what's the rush?"

"Exactly," Mom said. "We come out here to get away from the rat race."

"I'm Jerry," he said, standing and extending his hand.

"Angie Woods," Mom said, shaking his hand, "and this is my son, Jordan."

We set out again. Jerry looked older than Mom with his long gray hair, but he was in decent shape. It was pretty obvious he liked her, and I thought she might like him, too, so I walked a little ahead so they could talk. She likes to talk on the trail more than I do.

Mom has a date every now and then but no steady boyfriend, at least that I know about. Once or twice a week she goes out to meet a friend at Starbucks, or so she says. Sometimes she gets back late and I wonder if the friend is a guy, and if so, why she doesn't just tell me about him. Her business, I guess.

When we reached the viewpoint near the summit, Mom checked her watch and broke into a smile.

"One hour, fifty-eight minutes," she said. "Rainier, here we come!" She and Jerry slapped hands and we complimented her. I was glad she was back in shape and feeling better about herself.

We found some comfortable rocks to sit on and dug out our lunches. Some other hikers were talking on cell phones. Mom and Jerry shook their heads. She never let me bring my phone or my iPod, and had given me a lecture about not shutting out the sounds of nature and all that.

While eating, we enjoyed the view. The east side of Mount Si is a cliff, and you end up looking almost straight down at the green pastures of the Snoqualmie River Valley. It all looks so peaceful from up high. In the distance we could see Lake Washington, Seattle, and the Olympic Mountains.

"Stupendous," Mom said. "Absolutely magnificent."

I turned to her with a raised eyebrow, and she smiled. Every time we take a hike and reach a viewpoint, Mom feels obliged to declare how beautiful the scene is. I tease her that she's been looking up words in the thesaurus. The first time I called her on it, she looked sort of hurt, but then she laughed at herself and it's become a running joke. She really does appreciate beauty, which is cool, but now I think she makes her declarations just to get a reaction.

She'd made us turkey sandwiches on rye, and we also had some crackers and candy. She'd said we needed something salty to keep away leg cramps, and something with sugar for energy. Whatever—I just like that stuff because it tastes good.

A gray jay landed next to Jerry. "Look how fat this bird is!" he said. "People feed the little beggars all day. By August they're so fat it's a wonder they can fly."

He held out his hand, and when the bird landed there, he rewarded it with a crumb. "Contributing to the delinquency of a jaybird," Mom said.

When I was done eating, I told Mom I was going to hit the Haystack. The real summit of Si loomed a couple hundred feet over our heads. The first week we came, when I told Mom I was going to the top, she tapped the sign that read, "Haystack Scramblers, Please Use Extreme Caution." I rolled my eyes and went up it with ease.

Of course, I'm a rock climber. Most of the folks I see on the Haystack don't know what the hell they're doing, and I guess there have been a lot of broken bones and even deaths. My only worry is that one of those idiots will fall on me. I mean, I've seen them coming down, facing out, away from the rock, eyes all wide with terror, just looking to become a wilderness statistic. I politely tell them it's safer if they turn around and face the rock, but a lot of them ignore me or tell me to mind my own business. Don't mean to be rude, but I think a fat old guy falling on me *is* my business.

On top of the stack, I waved down to Mom and Jerry. I saw about thirty hikers sitting around the big lower summit area, but there were only two other climbers—a couple in their twenties—who were on the stack with me. They were both lean and fit and moved up the rock quickly and expertly. We chatted a little bit and quietly laughed at some of the folks we saw below, laboring up the rock. Scrambling up is safer than scrambling down, when gravity tries to give you a push. We thought some of them might learn that the hard way.

I descended the Haystack in about five minutes. Mom and Jerry were waiting and we headed down the trail. We'd gone about a quarter mile, and I was right behind Jerry, when he ripped a fart.

"Oops," he said. "Those bean burritos get me every time."

Mom gave me a look but we didn't say anything. Then a couple minutes later, Jerry ripped another.

"Sounds like you have a trumpet up your butt," I said.

"Jordan!" Mom snapped.

"Sorry."

"No, that's okay," Jerry said, "although I thought it was more of an alto sax."

Hard not to like a guy who can laugh at himself. Still, I passed him as soon as I could to get out of range. Mom said, "If you can't fart on a mountain, where can you fart?"

He laughed. "You're a kindred soul, Angie."

What he didn't know was that Mom was just being nice. She's kind of a nut for neatness and politeness, and requires me to say "excuse me" if I fart in the house, so I knew that she wasn't thrilled by Jerry's burrito bombs, even if we were on a mountain.

It only took us an hour to hike down. Nearing the trailhead, I told Mom I was going to run to the car. I said goodbye to Jerry and took off. Wanted to give them some space again, in case they felt like exchanging phone numbers, stuff like that.

I was sitting on the car trunk drinking water when Mom walked up a few minutes later, without Jerry. "So did you get a date?" I asked.

"No, changed my mind about Jerry," she said with a sour smile. "A man who farts repeatedly in public must be an absolute nightmare in private."

FIVE

He had enormous hopes for the future.
He considered: mucus egg congestions are
related to radiant sea creatures via
indecipherable links of change.

—Thomas McGuane

A few days later I got hit in the head by an octagon. It hung above my head in math class, and just fell—a reminder that gravity always wins in the end, sometimes gradually, sometimes with an avalanche.

Mrs. Morris, my teacher, laughed and apologized. The octagon was made out of paper and dangled next to a truncated square pyramid, a pentagonal prism, and various other colorful geometric shapes. She joked that I was lucky. "If the tetrahedron hit you, you'd probably be in the hospital."

Her classroom is in Building Three at Mountain View, but the windows face the courtyard. She has film posters from *A Beautiful Mind* and *The Shawshank Redemption* on the wall—the main characters were numbers men, she said—along with other math-related posters. One chart with a big headline on top caught my attention: "When Are We Ever Going to Have to Use This?" Which was a question a lot of students asked in math class. The chart listed careers on the horizontal axis and math subjects on the vertical, and dots where they intersected. There were a lot of dots.

I had looked over the chart carefully when we'd had a little free time at the end of class the first week of school. Sadly, Professional Rock Climber and Second Story Man weren't among the careers listed.

I was one of the few juniors in Precalculus. One of the other juniors was Matt Bird, who had been my best friend in middle school. We get along okay now, mostly because I make an effort to keep him in my universe. He's not a sports guy unless you count video games, and he's a little chunky. As I gravitated more toward the gym and other athletes, we'd drifted farther apart. No one's fault, really—though he blamed me. When I started sitting with A.J. and the other jocks at lunch, Matt looked at me like I was a traitor.

Anyway, math was my favorite subject, and it's really

like climbing at its core—you're just trying to solve problems, whether equations or route-finding. I can get totally focused and lose track of time working a good math problem, just the way I can when I'm working a wall. An hour passes like a few minutes.

On that day, Mrs. Morris asked if anyone wanted to do the first homework problem on the overhead projector. I raised my hand.

"Jordan," she said, "show us how it's done."

I walked to the front. Just like with teaching belaying at the gym, I was nervous the first few times but after a while felt very comfortable. A fair percentage of the grade in her class is participation, and I wanted to keep my straight-A math average intact.

I copied the problem on the sheet and put it over the light. "So there it is. I cancelled the like terms and factored this out," I said, pointing to the numerals and representative letters. "I think I have the right answer."

"Let's check his numerator," Mrs. Morris told the class. "Matt, what did you get?"

"Same thing," he said. "But I had an extra step. I think Jordo cheated." We smiled at each other.

"Yes, Jordan, you skipped a step but managed to get the right answer anyway," Mrs. Morris said. "Explain what you did."

I tried to explain it as clearly as I could, but I lost most of the class. "It's a redundant step the other way," I concluded.

"Like, I don't get how you did that at all."

"Me, neither."

Mrs. Morris said, "The step may be redundant, but it clarifies the process." She was smiling at me and shook her head a little. "Rather elegant maneuver, Jordan."

"Thanks."

We did some more of the homework problems, then Mrs. Morris went over perfect cubes. She assigned textbook problems for the remainder of the period. "No calculators on these," she added, "because the calculator won't give you as precise a number. Precision is important. If you're building an airplane I'll be flying on with my family, I don't want you estimating. I want exact numbers."

That got a chuckle and we started on the problems. The first two were easy, though some students around me struggled. "Way back when math was easy," Mrs. Morris told another student, "you added three plus two and got five. People love that and want to stay there, but that won't work with square roots. You can't add them unless the radicals are exactly the same."

I smiled, feeling superior. Then I got lost in a problem about the IRS allowing businesses to take an accelerated depreciation, each year deducting ten percent of the building's value at the beginning of the year. The sequencing required was pretty basic and I finished in five minutes. Mom's an accountant, so I'd have to tell her about that one, I thought.

Reading the next problem, I grinned and said, "No way!"

"What's up?" Matt asked.

"This problem is about climbing," I said. "So cool."

"Yeah, so cool," he said sarcastically. Climbing was still a sore spot with us, the cause of the rift from his point of view, and I wished I'd just kept my mouth shut. I wish that pretty often, actually.

The problem read, *Suppose you are climbing a mountain. Distance from the summit is a function of time. Speed varies, so you can't find the distance simply by multiplying rate by time. You can, however, use the concept of limit.* It went on to explain the concept and then I had to apply it. No sweat.

I was in the middle of the third problem when the bell rang. Math's the only class where the bell ever catches me off guard, and the only class I don't want to leave.

．　．　．

My last class of the day was Junior English with Mr. McGinnis. I'd been keeping an eye out for Juana all day, but Mountain View is a big campus. I figured I'd just have to look for her again at You So Mighty.

Then she walked into my English class. How cool is that? She had a registration form she handed to McGinnis, and he added her to his attendance book and said, "Welcome to class, um, Miss Miller. Is your first name pronounced how I think it's pronounced?"

"I go by Juana."

"Great. Welcome, Juana. We keep a journal in here

so get a separate notebook for that. Everybody, write in your journals while I take attendance. Topics are on the board."

There was an open seat next to me and I had to restrain myself from waving to her. Fortunately, she spotted me and smiled. I forgot to breathe for a moment, then I was okay.

"How's the first day going?" I asked in a whisper.

"Good. You were right, most of the teachers are okay."

"What's up with your name that freaked out McGinnis?"

"Tell you after class," she said with a little smile. "Want to go to Starbucks?"

"Yeah, sure."

We were starting *Snow Falling on Cedars*, our last novel of the year, and Mr. McGinnis told us to take notes while he gave us background on the book. "I think you'll like this," he said. "It's set in the San Juan Islands, so it's fairly local. How many of you have been to the islands?"

About half the class raised hands, including me. Juana didn't raise her hand and asked me, "Nice?"

"Yeah, and Orcas Island even has a couple of mountains."

McGinnis said that the writer of the book, David Guterson, did a great job capturing the feel of the islands. "The descriptions are wonderful, but the novel might move a bit slowly for some of you. That's a good thing, in my opinion. Slow down. Enjoy the scenery. You can miss life if you run through it too fast."

Juana whispered, "I like this guy."

"He's okay," I said, wondering why the adults in my life were hitting me over the head with the "slow down and smell the roses" theme lately. I was also feeling illogically jealous that Juana was growing fond of Mr. McGinnis, even though I knew she didn't like him *that* way. I mean, he was old and fat, not a lean mean climber dude like me. No competition.

"The novel also explores a nasty incident in American history," McGinnis continued. "How many of you have heard of concentration camps?"

Just about every hand flew up, and Mike Albert mentioned the Nazi concentration camps.

"Yes, those are rather famous. How many of you were aware that the United States had similar camps?"

No hands.

"Well, we did, and it was shameful, in my opinion. Concentration camps bring to mind the Holocaust, so it's probably stretching the point to call them that. Internment camps is the usual reference. They were in California, Arizona, various other states, about ten in all. The residents were Japanese Americans." He put an emphasis on the last word. "Yes, most were U.S. citizens."

He explained that the fear after the bombing of Pearl Harbor was similar to that of 9/11. "At least we didn't put all Muslim-Americans in camps," he said, "although the government compromised the civil rights of many.

Freedom and security require a difficult balancing act in this day and age."

Mohammad Rizwan raised his hand and said, "My brother was taken off a plane right after 9/11." Mohammad is a funny and smart guy who goes by Mo, but he wasn't laughing then. "They interrogated him for like two hours. He was pissed."

"Understandably so," McGinnis said. "And that raises an interesting point. Why was your brother signaled out? Why were Japanese Americans singled out during World War Two, and not Italian and German Americans? After all, we were also at war with Italy and Germany."

After a few seconds, Juana said, "Because Germans and Italians are white."

Everyone stared at her. "Bluntly put, Miss Miller," McGinnis said, "and entirely correct. This very fact was pointed out by a brave newspaper editor on Whidbey Island—the only editor on the entire West Coast who took a stand against the Japanese imprisonment. He received death threats. In *Snow*, Guterson bases a character on him. The protagonist's father."

We read part of the first chapter until the bell rang. As we walked down the hall, I said, "The parking lot here is impossible to exit for like at least fifteen minutes. Starbucks is close. Want to walk over?"

"Yeah, let me drop my books in my car and we'll walk."

We headed across campus through light showers of

rain, following the rest of the throng. She walked fast, like me. I also liked that she was a couple of inches shorter. I'd had crushes on a few girls in middle school who were about my size at the time, but now they looked down on me, in every sense.

The final good sign was that she liked caramel macchiatos, too. We nabbed a couple of soft chairs near the window. "So what's up with your name?" I asked.

She smiled and sipped her coffee. "Juana is short for Marijuana."

I was about to take a sip myself, but that stopped me. "No shit?"

"I shit thee not. You know what *my* parents were doing when they hooked up."

"So your parents were hippie types?"

"About twenty years late, but yeah, that describes how they were at the time. Part of Eugene never left the sixties. They met at a health food store where they both worked, and they hit it off and shacked up right away. I was around for more than a year before they got married, a little fact they don't like to discuss. They did smoke a fair amount of weed, and they say they liked the way the word marijuana sounded—four flowing syllables. It's a wonder I don't have brain damage."

"They gradually straightened out?"

"Rather suddenly, actually. My dad is a good businessman and worked his way up to manager of a store, then owner, and then he started a little chain of health food stores around Eugene. He made a lot of money when they spread to Portland. Now he's up here opening a few new stores."

She paused for a sip and I took the opportunity to thank the gods for new health food stores.

"So anyway," she continued, "when they first started making good money, they took a hard turn toward respectability. They got married, became best friends with Jesus, began wearing suits, the whole thing. The Great Right Shift, I call it. Started when I was about five and has been going strong ever since."

"Wow, what a change."

"Yup, and they want me right there with them. That's one reason we don't get along so great. A few years ago they even tried to get me to legally change my name to Mary Jane. I told them to forget it."

"Juana's a cool name," I said, "but I bet you'll get teased when it gets around what your full name is."

"I can handle it, although I prefer not to explain. How about your parents?"

"It's just me and my mom."

"Your parents divorced?"

"No, my dad died when I was young."

"Sorry, Jordan." She felt bad and put her hand on mine. I'd been thinking about trying to hold her hand when we walked over, but it didn't seem right. Now it did.

We didn't talk for a while, just sipped our drinks and watched the rain fall harder outside. I didn't feel like talking about my dad—it made me feel bad thinking about him, and right then, holding hands with a new friend, I was feeling good.

SIX

I was in a malevolent place; a tangible hostility enclosed me as if the air had been charged with static electricity. This was not the playground we had walked into so long ago.

—Joe Simpson

On the second Friday in May, A.J. and I looked around at lunch and thought that it was too nice a day for school. We decided to skip our afternoon classes and go to Index Town Walls.

"Can't miss track practice," Casey said between bites of his burger.

"Come on, Case," A.J. said. "I won the hundred, the

two hundred, and anchored our win in the four-hundred relay yesterday. I deserve a day off."

"Coach'll be pissed."

"It's not like I'm just gonna be sitting around watching TV," A.J. argued. "I'll still be working out."

"Climbing ain't working out," Casey said, and threw a French fry at me. I threw it back. Down the table Billy Briggs said something to another player and I heard the phrase "Monkey Boy." He's a jerk and we don't get along. I wondered if he knew Casey and I were kidding around.

"We should stay overnight," A.J. said. "Supposed to be nice tomorrow, too. We could camp by the river and climb another couple of routes in the morning before heading back."

I was nodding. No one ever had to talk me into climbing a crag. I called Mom on my cell and told her the plan— well, the part about climbing that afternoon and staying overnight. Skipped the part about cutting out of school early.

"Just be careful out there," she said. "Tell A.J. if anything happens to you, he'll have to answer to me."

"No worries, Mom. Thanks."

I debated asking Juana if she wanted to come along. She had a different lunch, so I couldn't talk to her then. We hadn't had an official date or anything yet, though we'd talked a lot while climbing at the gym. Asking her to camp overnight might be too much. Maybe I could ask her if she wanted to just drive out this afternoon, or tomorrow, just meet us there to climb. Too much info for a text, so I called her cell and left a message.

A.J. always parked his car at a friend's house a block away from school, since they shut the parking lot gates after school starts and there's no way to drive out until the end of the day. Escaping by foot is another matter. We walked to the back of school and headed for the wire fence. Brockman was staked out and chased us in his golf cart, which was fun, but we outran him and climbed the fence. Everybody knows A.J., so there was a good chance he'd get busted for this. I might get away with it, though. We'd find out on Monday.

A.J. drove to his house first, then mine. We got a tent, rope, and the rest of our climbing gear, along with a cooler and cooking stuff. By twelve thirty we were headed across the Highway 2 trestle toward cow country. We'd just finished the curve to the southeast when we saw a tall guy with a gray-brown beard and glasses hitchhiking on the side of the road. He looked sort of familiar from a distance and I recognized him as we passed.

"Hey, it's Zenny," I said. "Pull over, A.J."

He pulled onto the shoulder and backed up. Zenny was a fellow climber we'd gotten to know out at Index. Unlike some of the other older climbers, he was always friendly and willing to share information about crags.

"Hey, guys," he said when he saw it was us. "No school today?"

"The day is clear and the crags are calling," I said.

"Yeah, I hear them, too," he said, folding into the back seat with his pack.

We pulled back onto the highway. "You don't have a car, Zenny?" A.J. asked in his innocently direct way.

"No, the only place I go regularly is Snohomish to pick up supplies, and that's within walking distance. During the warm months I'll head out to Index a couple times a week to climb, and I'll either catch a ride with friends or hitch."

"Where do you live?" I asked.

"Aboard a houseboat on Ebey Slough," he said. "It's about a half mile north of where you picked me up."

"My dad has a friend who lives on a sailboat at the Everett Marina," A.J. said. "We sailed with him a few times. Seems like a cool way to live."

"I like it. My boat doesn't move, but I have a kayak to get around. My only means of transportation, other than my feet. And thumb."

"You ever think of moving your boat over to the marina?" I asked. "Be closer to town and all that?"

"No, I like the quiet life where I'm at. The marina also charges moorage fees, whereas I'm in unincorporated Snohomish County, which is free."

"Nice," A.J. said, "but it's probably hard to meet hotties on the slough, especially if you don't have a car."

Zenny laughed. "I suppose there is a hottie shortage," he said. "I've had the same girlfriend for going on ten years, so I really haven't noticed."

"Yeah?" A.J. said. "I thought you were like a Zen monk or something."

"No, I spent a few months in a monastery a long time ago, that's all. Made the mistake of telling some of my climbing buddies, who wondered where I'd gone. They gave me the nickname Zenny. It stuck."

"Really," I said. "We heard you were a monk for years."

"Nope, never a monk. Part of me is attracted to the austere life they lead, but I also have an artistic temperament that bridles at order and authority."

"Pretty wild how rumors get taken for fact," A.J. said. "What's your girlfriend's name? Is she a climber?"

A.J. was just being his curious and friendly self, and I thought it was a fairly innocent question. But Zenny looked very uncomfortable. "No offense," he said, "but I like to keep my private life private."

A.J. and I glanced at each other, then shrugged. To change the subject, I said, "I'm surprised you don't go into Everett for supplies. Isn't that closer than Snohomish?"

"About the same walking distance," he said. "But I try to avoid Everett."

"Why?" I asked.

"Bad karma."

"What do you mean?" A.J. asked. We were both feeling a little defensive. I mean, we'd lived in Everett all our lives.

"The massacre," he said. "Bloody Sunday. It's a collective bad karma. I know it sounds strange, but I can sense it when I'm over there. Makes me a little sad and anxious and angry, and those are feelings I prefer to avoid."

"What massacre?" I asked.

"You never heard of the Everett Massacre?"

"No."

"Well, I shouldn't be surprised. Most of the town would prefer that nasty bit of history to just disappear, so they probably don't talk about it much in the schools."

"I think Mr. Powers talked about it in American History last year," A.J. said. "I was spacing out a little so I don't remember too much about what he said. Something about labor unions, right?"

"Yes, it involved union issues. The massacre took place at high noon on Sunday, November 5th, 1916."

"Whoa, back a ways," I said. "And you think Everett is still carrying baggage from that?"

"Oh, yes. Powerful families and politicians continue to deny it every day, so the karmic power continues. Don't get me wrong, Everett has come a long way in recent years. Wonderful waterfront and downtown, nice event center, all that. But it will never be a great city until it acknowledges its sordid past. There's no monument to the massacre, and they like to refer to it as an embarrassing incident that happened a long time ago. That doesn't cut it."

"What happened, exactly?" I asked.

"Well, Everett has one pulp mill on the waterfront now, but it used to have dozens. And they were terrible places. Most mill workers put in fourteen hours a day for lousy wages, and many died from accidents and what they called 'cedar asthma,' caused by all the dust in the air. If you had five or six fingers left after a dozen years in the mills, you were lucky."

"Holy shit!" A.J. said.

"Yeah, it was bad. So the Industrial Workers of the World, known formally as the IWW and informally as Wobblies, tried to help the workers organize a union. They came to Everett several times. The day before Halloween that year, forty-one Wobblies came to Everett from Seattle to talk to the workers. They gathered downtown, and were moved by sheriff's deputies a couple blocks away. They argued, and so the deputies transported them to Beverly Park, where they were forced to run the gauntlet—meaning, run between two lines of thugs who beat them with clubs. Just dumb luck that no one was killed that night. It was a bloody mess."

"Happy Halloween," I said quietly, picturing the scene.

"Right. So a week later two ships loaded with Wobblies came up from Seattle, a bigger presence to get their message across. The Snohomish County Sheriff was a guy named Donald McRae, who was of course in the pocket of the mill owners. They spread rumors that the Wobblies were coming up to burn the town, kill people, like they were terrorists, when in fact the Wobblies just wanted to spread the word of union brotherhood. It's ironic that Everett is a major union town now. All your teachers are in a union, along with the Boeing workers and many others. Go figure."

"This is pissing me off," A.J. said, "and it was almost a hundred years ago!"

"So what happened when the ships came up from Seattle?" I asked.

"They tried to dock at Pier One. McRae had 'deputized' a couple hundred angry and fearful townsfolk, all armed to the teeth. As the first boat, the steamer Verona, tried to land, McRae yelled, 'You can't land here!' A Wobbly supposedly yelled back, 'The hell we can't!' And then there was a shot. And then many shots."

We waited for more, but Zenny didn't say anything. When I looked in the rearview mirror, his head was bowed and he was chanting quietly. It didn't sound like English.

Finally he looked up. "The official count was two deputies killed and twenty wounded, including McRae. The official count also says that five Wobblies were killed and twenty-seven wounded. Unofficially, it's speculated that a couple dozen Wobblies were killed. Some of the deputies later confessed to tying rocks to the bodies and sinking them so the official body count wouldn't be so alarming. They couldn't escape the word 'massacre,' though."

We were quiet for a while as we drove through Gold Bar, looking at the Cascades rising before us. Then Zenny finished the story. "I grew up in Billings, Montana," he said. "After my senior year in high school I went hiking and scrambling alone in the Bighorn Mountains in eastern Wyoming, not too far from home. One day I lost my way and went up a canyon south of where I wanted to be. By the time I realized my mistake, the sun was heading down, and I camped in a draw between two ridges."

Again he was quiet for about a minute or so, like he was gathering strength or something.

"It was the worst night of my life. I felt blood and death all around me, evil spirits, and I saw a ghost—a bloody Indian holding a spear. I got sick and was a wreck all night, and of course I didn't sleep. Later I learned that Federal troops had massacred a tribe in the general vicinity of where I was hiking."

We looked at each other with our mouths open. "I'm part Lummi," A.J. said. "My mom's people didn't have anything that bad happen. I get it, though."

"Well, after I moved here I read about the Everett Massacre, and one day I paddled my kayak over to check out Pier One," he continued. "I was enjoying the paddle for a while. Riding the ebb tide past the highway bridges, watching the herons and shorebirds, cruising past Jetty Island, the marina, the naval base. A really fine day.

"Then I came to the industrial area where Pier One is located, and the sunlight seemed to fade. I felt exactly like I had in the Bighorns, and I puked over the side of the kayak. Maybe I'm oversensitive. Don't take my word for it, check it out yourselves. But I like to avoid Everett."

We were almost to Index when he said, "You can't escape the past by pretending it doesn't exist."

SEVEN

I will not become an obstacle to myself.

—Agrippinus

We turned left toward Index a few minutes later, drove a quarter-mile or so down the road, then crossed the bridge over the Skykomish River. The town is small, maybe a few hundred people. We stopped at the general store for water, firewood, and food, and A.J. tried to talk Zenny into buying us some beer. He politely refused, and we drove about a mile along the river, back west, to a little dirt parking lot.

Five other cars were in the lot, about what we expected. Index Town Walls are the heart of trad climbing in the area, so it can get crowded on nice weekends. We guessed there would be another ten cars or more by late afternoon.

We walked back across the road and set up our two tents in an informal campground overlooking the river. We knew other climbers would be camping there and wanted to get the primo spot. We laughed at Zenny when he suggested that we take a less than fantastic spot, as an act of loving kindness toward unmet friends. He shrugged and smiled when we said no.

Shouldering our packs, we hiked up the path next to the parking lot. A bullet-riddled stop sign stood in front of the railroad tracks. We looked both ways and crossed quickly, because fast-moving trains came through here all the time. No one had ever been killed climbing at Index, but a few had been killed by trains.

We walked across talus and came to the path that ran parallel to the Lower Wall, which was five hundred feet high and maybe a quarter mile wide, one of the best crags anywhere. Zenny said he was going to scramble around the dihedral at Roger's Corner. We told him we'd see him later and continued east on the path to the Great Northern Slab.

We decided to start with a relatively easy route called Taurus. We stretched a little and prepared our harnesses, sixty-meter rope, and protection. Protection is stuff like small-wired nuts, chocks, and spring-loaded camming devices. You keep them handy on your harness along with "quickdraws," which are two carabiners attached with a loop of webbing. The lead climber places protection as he climbs, locks a carabiner from the quickdraw on it, then passes the rope through the carabiner on the other end of the webbing. This keeps the rope off the rocks.

The other climber belays his partner from below while the lead climber goes up the wall and places protection. If the lead climber falls, he'd only go as far as his last protection—in theory. Sometimes protection pulls loose, and it's not something any climber wants to test.

Anyway, when the lead climber gets to a ledge where he's safe, he then builds an anchor and belays his partner over that segment—called a pitch. That second climber removes the protection on the way up, and then you repeat the process on the rest of the pitches.

A.J. liked to compare climbing protection to sex protection. "A horny guy wants to get *into* the crack without putting on a rubber," he said, "and a climber wants to go *up* a crack without putting in a cam. Pausing for any protection sucks big-time."

"So does knocking up your girlfriend, contracting a disease, and falling to your death," I argued.

I've been placing cams and stuff for so many years it's fairly automatic. A.J. obviously hated placing protection, and when he led, the gaps between his gear were much too big. He shrugged me off when I criticized him for this, and I finally told him I wouldn't climb with him anymore if he wasn't more careful.

He's been better since, but still has a reckless side. That's one reason why, despite being a great athlete, he's just a little better than the average climber. Another reason is that he doesn't like small holds even if they're solid, and still another is that he tends to rely too much on his upper body strength. Climbing is really more of a foot thing, which is why girl climbers like Juana are usually better than big strong guys—they don't wear themselves out doing pull-ups on holds.

"Let me lead this one, Jordo," A.J. said when we had our helmets and harnesses on.

"Sure," I said, and grabbed the belay device while he tied the rope to his harness. Usually we "leapfrogged," meaning we alternated as lead climbers. But if he wanted to lead the whole way on this one, I was okay with that.

"On belay?" he asked.

"Belay on."

"Climbing."

He went up the crag well. We had an interesting traverse under a roof, and a tricky step-across move, and then it was a fairly easy climb to the top. We rappelled down from an anchor. We had time for one more climb, and there was one I'd had my eye on for a while called Virgin on the Ridiculous. Few climbers tried it, but it looked interesting to me. And it was close by.

"You go for that one, Jordo," A.J. said. "Out of my league."

We went over and he belayed me. Some decent cracks, but they ran out, and I had to use all my skills to make use of small holds between the cracks. I was totally focused and, for some reason, felt that my body knew where to go and would get me to the top. I've heard basketball players talk about the zone, and that's what it was like. I couldn't miss.

I topped out and A.J. cheered down below. He was really pumped for me, and hugged me and slapped me on the back when I got down. I understood why Casey said he was such a good teammate.

. . .

Back at the campground, we noticed a third tent. Zenny showed up a few minutes later, and A.J. told him about Virgin on the Ridiculous. Then he tried to talk him into buying beer again. "Come on, dude!" he said. "We've got to celebrate Jordan's wall!"

"A brilliant accomplishment," Zenny said with a smile, "but I'm still not buying you beer."

Not long after, the owners of the third tent showed up—Jake and Steve, a couple of climbers from Monroe in their early twenties. We knew them a little, and A.J. made the pitch for beer again, offering to pay for theirs, too. They said sure and he went back with them to the general store. I half-expected Zenny to voice an objection, but he just relaxed in his tent, reading a book he brought along called *Silence of the Heart*.

While they were gone, I started a fire and prepared dinner in the big frying pan I brought along. I was pretty good with basic climbing fare like pancakes, eggs, and mishmash stew, which was on the menu tonight. I browned the ground beef while chopping up an onion, a carrot, a tomato, and mushrooms—my climbing knife comes in handy. Then I poured off the grease and stirred the veggies into the pan along with two big cans of baked beans.

Dinner was ready by the time they got back, and there was enough for all of us. Zenny declined both the stew and the beer and munched on cheese and crackers, then excused himself and went back to his tent and book.

"So," Jake said after we'd eaten and cleaned up, "I heard you did Virgin on the Ridiculous."

"Yeah, a nice route," I said.

"Sure that's the route you did?" Steve asked. "We haven't been able to knock off that one."

"I'm sure, yeah."

"Damn right," A.J. said. "I'm a witness. It was unbelievably hairy."

"I thought you were mostly a gym climber?" Steve said.

"I do both."

"Gym climbing just don't compare to crag climbing," Jake said. "It's like comparing a VW Bug to an Indy Car."

"Or football practice to a game," A.J. added.

"At the gym," I said, wanting to be on their side, "I tell the climbers they're not getting a true appreciation for the sport. They need to hit the crags for that."

"Most gym climbers don't understand the risk involved," Steve said. "Or just the everyday realities out here."

"Yellow jackets and slippery moss," Jake nodded. "Not things you find in a gym."

"Or rattlesnakes," Steve added.

"Dude, there are no rattlesnakes on this side of the Casades!" A.J. said, and we all laughed.

"Well," Jake concluded, "indoor climbing is a sporting hobby, crag climbing is a lifestyle." He raised his beer. "Here's to the lifestyle!"

"The lifestyle!" we said, and drank down the rest of our beers. When everybody cracked a fresh can, Jake turned to me and said, "Congrats on Virgin, Jordan." He didn't say it like he meant it, but raised his beer again. "Let's celebrate that achievement. We guzzle on three. Ready—one, two, three!"

We all guzzled a whole beer. I immediately felt light-headed. We didn't guzzle again, but we kept drinking. I wanted to stop, but Jake kept handing me beers and saying stuff like, "Drink up, it's Virgin on the Ridiculous what a lightweight you are!" And so I kept drinking.

My laughter sounded strange and distant after a while, and everything seemed funny. When a group of rafters floated by on the river, I jumped up and shouted, "Hey, there's a full moon over the Skykomish!" Then I dropped my pants and turned my butt cheeks to them. A.J. and the other guys whooped and joined me.

That was about the last thing I remember before passing out. I woke up a couple hours later, after dark, and everything was spinning. I was barely able to get out of the tent and over to the river before puking. I heard Jake and Steve laughing a little while I sucked in greedy gulps of air and waited for the world to steady—which it refused to do.

"You okay?" A.J. asked quietly from the tent door.

"No, dude."

"I have some Tylenol. Take some later, I'll leave it by your pad."

"Thanks," I said, thinking, *Yes, thanks so much for getting that beer and telling those jerks about my climb. I really appreciate that, buddy.*

Zenny unzipped his tent and came over with some paper towels and a bottle of water. I thanked him weakly.

"Probably not a good time for a lecture on moderation, huh, Jordo?"

"God, I don't know why I drank that much. I'll never drink another beer as long as I live."

"Think I made that same promise in college a few times," he said with a little laugh.

"I don't know if I'm gonna be able to climb tomorrow."

"Don't even think about it. You're going to have a hangover and be weak as a newborn."

"Why the hell did I do this to myself?"

"Rhetorical question?"

"Yeah ... I did it because I'm an idiot."

"You don't have to impress anyone, Jordan. Climb routes because you want to climb them. Have a few beers if you feel like it. Just make sure it's your decision."

In the morning, my head felt like a drum that some asshole wouldn't stop beating. My mouth was dry and I felt as dehydrated as if I'd climbed a desert spire. The effort to sit up and drink from my water bottle almost destroyed me. I couldn't climb out of the tent, much less a crag.

Everyone else was already up and eating breakfast—through the tent netting I could see their backs around the fire. Jake looked over at me and said, "Hey Jordan, why don't you prove to us you did Virgin on the Ridiculous? You up for a repeat performance?"

I didn't answer, just lay back on my pad. I used my backpack for a pillow, so my head was propped slightly and I could still see them.

Zenny said, "That was a lousy thing you did."

"Why don't you shut up?" Jake replied.

"Just don't pull that crap again."

"Hey, I didn't force the beers down his throat."

"Just about. You took advantage of a high school kid because you're jealous."

A second of silence, then Jake stood and exploded into a tirade of curses and threats. A.J. was yelling for

Jake to chill and Steve was holding back his friend. Jake was staring daggers at Zenny, who had stood and was staring right back.

"I should kick your old weak ass!" Jake shouted.

"I don't want to fight you," Zenny said in his relaxed way, like he was discussing the breakfast menu. "But I'll defend myself if you attack me."

Jake thought it over. Steve pleaded for them to go, and after staring at Zenny for a few more seconds, Jake turned and walked off. I could hear him throwing stuff around and cursing as they packed up.

I slept a little while. A.J. woke me when he came into the tent to get some gear. "Zenny and I are going to do Breakfast of Champions," he said. "It's the route right next to Taurus that we were looking at yesterday. Then we'll come back and take off. Give you a couple more hours to recover."

"Okay."

"Sorry about the beers, Jordo. I shouldn't have let that happen."

"I'll get even."

He smiled and left with Zenny. About ten minutes later, I heard a car pull into the lot, then footsteps approaching the campground.

"Hello? Anybody home?"

Shit! I'd forgotten I'd invited Juana. For a second I considered hiding, but she might come over and look inside anyway—she was getting closer.

"Hey, Juana," I said. "I'm over here."

I managed to sit up and unzip the netting as she walked over. She took one look at me, then turned and looked at the impressive pile of beer cans nearby.

"A little under the weather?"

"Yeah, you could say that."

"How many did you have?"

"No idea," I said, "but I regret every one."

She laughed and squatted down so she could see me better. "God, Jordan."

"I know, I'm a lightweight."

"Well, literally. Alcohol is going to hit you a lot harder than a big guy."

"Yeah, that'd make a good math problem. 'Two men are drinking beers, one weighing one-forty and the other two-forty. How many sixteen-ounce beers can they consume before the little guy falls down and pukes?'"

"At least you haven't lost your sense of humor."

"No, not yet. Look, I'm obviously in no shape, but A.J. and Zenny went over to a crag. If you want to go over and do some scrambling…"

"That's okay. I'll stay with you. Is it safe in there for two? Did you puke in the tent?"

"No puke," I said, "but it's still pretty gross in here."

"I camp a lot," she said. "I can handle gross."

I scooted over to my pad to make room for her, and she stepped in and sat facing me on A.J.'s pad. "Not so bad," she said. She was smiling a little, and reached out and brushed some hair out of my eyes. "You're cute even when you're hungover."

Now normally, that would've been my cue to kiss her. But not with puke breath. Not if I ever wanted to kiss her again.

"You should rest," she said. "Go ahead, lie down. I think I'll take a nap myself. Do you want some Tylenol or anything?"

"Just had some a little while ago, thanks." I took a sip of water, then lay back on my pad and pack. Juana snuggled up next to me and held my hand, and I felt a little better.

"This is a nice spot," she said, looking out through the netting. "I like the sound of the river. And those are some dramatic mountains over there."

"That's Mount Index on the left and Persis on the right."

"Oh, I read a little about Index," she said. "That's the one where Jim Whittaker almost fell."

"Yeah, when he was climbing with his brother Lou when they were young. Had to jump for a hold. He barely made it, and he was like a six-five former basketball player."

"The crazy stuff people do in the mountains."

"Right, like drink beer."

She laughed, and then we were quiet, and soon we fell asleep.

EIGHT

*Brother, when you return to our village you must
tell our people that we must accept whatever it is
we are becoming. I have learned this and now I
will be all right. Sometimes we grow up to be like
everyone else, but sometimes we do not. People
are always afraid of turning into something
unusual, but they must not be afraid. We must
be happy with whatever we are becoming.*

—Jamake Highwater

A few days later after school, Juana and I were walking down the hall together when Billy Briggs came up behind her and stepped on her tail. I'd noticed she sometimes wore a long striped tail to school, attached to her pants or skirt, and so did some other kids. I hadn't asked her about it yet.

"Hey!" she said, stopping short. "Don't be an asshole!"

"Watch it Bill," said his buddy Mears, "that cat might scratch."

"Why don't you guys get lost?" I said.

They looked at each other, then at me. Briggs stepped close, looking down at me. Way down. He's about six-three.

"A.J. and Casey aren't around to protect you," he said, poking me in the chest. "So you better watch your mouth, Monkey Boy."

He poked my chest again and I slapped his hand away. He was winding up to punch me when Mr. Stenger, standing at his door, yelled, "Hey, cut it out! Right now!" He started walking toward us.

Briggs looked at Stenger, then back at me. He said, "Some other time, Monkey Boy. Count on it."

They walked away down the hall. Juana said, "Something tells me you have a history with that jerk."

"Yeah, none of it good."

"Want to talk about it?"

"I don't know," I shrugged.

Stenger asked if we were okay, and we said sure, no problem. "Looked like bullying," he said. "Let me know if there's another incident."

As we walked down the hall, Juana said, "I get curious when idiots mess with my tail. Come on, tell me about it!" She tickled me until I promised to tell all. We got a couple of waters from the vending machine, walked to the parking lot and sat in her car.

"Started freshman year," I began, and I remembered back when I was REALLY pint-sized...

. . .

Usually when the *Free Sasquatch* comes out, it's no big deal. I mean, everybody checks it out but nobody goes crazy. That all changed when the December issue was distributed. Students were literally fighting to get a copy, once word got around.

See, that was the issue when Phillip Thompson came out of the closet.

It was right there on the front page, a first-person account of what it's like to be a gay student at a modern American high school. And how he finally decided he wasn't going to pretend to be straight anymore.

Even the teachers were shocked. One said she thought it was the bravest thing she'd ever read. Another said he would've preferred a "don't ask, don't tell" approach. And another worried that Phillip might be beat up.

Mrs. Wendell, my social studies teacher, thought the controversial article created a teachable moment. She divided us up into groups to discuss it. I didn't have a problem with Phillip, but I said something about him being a fag who should shut up. I was small and thin, and sometimes other guys equate that with being gay for some reason. I wanted to make sure they knew I was hetero all the way.

At Mrs. Wendell's direction, we talked about the words "gay" and "fag," which students toss around all the time. A girl in my group named Mary Banville said, "It's okay to call a homosexual 'gay,' as long as you aren't saying it to be rude. If you use the word 'fag,' that isn't right. Fag is used more as a put-down."

"Sometimes it depends on the situation," Gary Nestor said. "I've heard that they call each other those words, like black guys call each other the N-word. It's like a 'Hey, dude' kind of thing, friendly, not mean."

I noticed most of the guys seemed pretty hostile to Phillip, while most of the girls were more understanding. Anyway, everybody was still talking about it at lunch that day. Most of us didn't know Phillip Thompson because he was a junior, but A.J. did. They were in a drama club together and sort of friends—of course, A.J. was friends with just about everybody. He got teased at lunch by Casey and the other football players.

"He seemed like a normal guy," A.J. said. "I didn't know he was a butt-hound."

"All those guys in the drama club are fags," Briggs said. He was at the other end of the table, a tall, handsome guy with a cleft chin. He played on the football and basketball teams and was almost as popular as A.J.

"I'm in drama club," A.J. said, looking over at Briggs, "and I'm not a fag. I think you're a pussy, though."

Briggs got up and charged over, his face one big snarl. Casey told me later that a fight between them had been coming for a while. Briggs was the freshman quarterback and didn't like all the attention A.J. got as star running back, moved up to varsity while Briggs was left behind. They'd had some words and shoving matches on the field a few times.

Briggs got in the first shot, but then A.J. ducked low and put a shoulder in Brigg's gut like he was a tackling dummy. He churned his legs hard. Briggs backpedaled, but A.J. clamped his hands around his legs and slammed him to the cafeteria floor. He was wailing on Brigg's face when Principal Denny and Brockman pulled him off.

They were both suspended for a few days. The next week, I was in the Building Five bathroom right before first period. I'm not a morning person and didn't really notice the football players hanging around outside the door. I was washing my hands when Phillip Thompson walked out of a stall. I sort of froze for a second, then went back to washing my hands, and was heading for the door when Briggs and two other guys walked into the bathroom.

"Look at this!" Billy said with a sneer. "The fags just got done with a hump session in the stall!"

"Hey, fuck you!" I yelled.

All my life I've gotten beaten up because I say stuff like that to bigger guys. They know I'm an easy target, and I guess they feel justified when I don't back down. Gotta stand up for myself, though, even if I don't stand tall. I'd usually get in a couple of punches and kicks before I was slammed to the ground, and I figured this would go the same way.

"We're not together," Phillip said. "I don't even know his name."

The football players hesitated, then snorted laughs. Billy said, "Well, you both look like fags to me," and started toward us. I threw my backpack at him and got in one shot to his ribs before he grabbed me by the neck. I shut my eyes and waited for the punches.

They never came. Casey Ragurski had walked into the bathroom, saw what was happening, and grabbed Briggs' arm as he was about to hit me. The sound of Briggs screaming in pain prompted me to open my eyes.

"Leave Jordo alone," Casey said, looking around the room while continuing to squeeze Briggs arm. "I don't care what you do with that fag, but don't touch Jordo. We're friends. Understand?"

"Leave Phillip alone, too," A.J. said, stepping out from behind Casey. "He's my friend. Anybody got a problem with that?"

There was silence for a few seconds, then the football players left. Briggs gave us all dirty looks, but didn't say anything.

"Guess I got a little problem with that," Casey said, smiling at A.J. Then he turned his gaze to Phillip. "I don't like fags."

"Lighten up, Case," A.J. said. "Phillip is cool."

Casey growled a little but didn't hassle Phillip, who seemed as resigned to getting the crap kicked out of him as I was. We were both so relieved we laughed a little as we walked out of the bathroom. And once it got around that A.J. thought Phillip was cool, that they were even friends, everybody left him alone.

. . .

"Right on," Juana said. "That was a good thing A.J. did."

"Yeah, it was. He's nice to everybody. I've never even seen him mad, except that time with Briggs. Casey says A.J. gets mad on the football field when he's tackled and guys take cheap shots when he's under the pile. I wouldn't know about that, though."

"So Billy Briggs still has it in for you."

"I think he sees me as unfinished business," I said. "He's knows Casey and A.J. would kick his ass, but he also senses I don't like to rely on them for protection."

"What a jerk," she said, shaking her head.

. . .

Juana and I decided to go climbing later at the gym. There wasn't much for me to do after eight except clean up, so that's when I did a lot of climbing. Pete, too. When I was putting my shoes on, waiting for Juana, he was belaying a guy who was struggling with a 5.8 route. "Is that a hold," Pete asked, "or an object of veneration?" The guy laughed and peeled off. Pete lowered him slowly to the mats, teasing him all the while.

When Juana came in, we did a couple of easy routes to warm up, then moved over to a 5.9 route. Marie came in late and we all talked a little. "Glad you're sticking with it," I said.

"I enjoy climbing here," she said. "It's a fabulous way to unwind after a tough day at the office. And I get bored just riding a stationary bike and doing aerobics."

Marie was headed to the bouldering area, but Pete came back in from the front counter and said he'd belay her. They walked over to the easier routes on the other side of the gym.

"They've had a couple of dates," I whispered.

"That's great," Juana said. "They look good together."

"And she's about his age. That's a first for Pete."

"You gotta grow up sometime."

On the other side of the gym, Marie was starting a 5.2 route. She was about ten feet up when we heard Pete's booming voice. "Marie," he said, "you have an exquisite ass."

"Pete," she shot back over her shoulder, "you ARE an exquisite ass."

"Haa!" he laughed. "A woman who knows me! I think I'm in love."

. . .

Juana and I were still laughing about that after Pete and Marie left. "I can't believe he told my fourth grade teacher she has an exquisite ass," I said, shaking my head.

"Yes, such a romantic."

As Juana and I became good friends and felt closer,

we'd naturally held hands and hugged a few times, but I hadn't kissed her yet. Either there was somebody around at the gym or I had puke breath—whatever, it hadn't seemed right. But tonight I was determined.

"Do you like swings?" I asked.

"Sure."

"Good. Grab that rope over there." While she tied her harness loop to the rope, I tied mine to the one next to her. "Now we swing!" I said, pushing hard off the wall with my feet. Once you get some momentum, you can go pretty far and high.

Juana got the hang of it right away, and was soon flying around and squealing. We bumped each other accidentally a few times, then not so accidentally. I thought I might have hurt her a little with one hip shot, so I apologized.

"Forget that," she said, swinging above me, "I just want to get even."

"Take your best shot."

She pushed off a wall hard and came at me feet first, nailing me right in the butt.

"That hurt!" I yelled, though it didn't hurt that much. I grabbed her harness on my next pass, and we swung together a few times, laughing. We were looking into each other's eyes and the ropes were settling down, and she leaned forward with her eyes shut. And I kissed her.

NINE

Well, we knocked the bastard off.

—Sir Edmund Hillary
on climbing Mt. Everest

The third Thursday of each month is Buccaneer Night at You So Mighty. When I walked in, Pete was standing beside a ladder in the northwest corner, working on a new "Masato-piece." That's what he called the 5.15 wall area in the northwest corner of the gym, the one with the daunting overhang, tiny holds, and wide-open spaces in-between.

Wearing a black beret and standing there with his

chin in his hand, Pete really did look like an artist. He rarely changed the other routes in the gym, but it was a tradition to alter the 5.15 on Buccaneer night and watch Masato Takasuki take the first crack at it. He hardly ever topped out the first time. Usually it took him a week or two to solve the problems Pete constructed. But in all the years I'd been climbing at You So Mighty, Masato had only failed to top out within the month a few times.

"I try to create a very challenging climb, but not an impossible one," Pete explained. "I know Masato's capabilities, but it's still difficult to strike the right balance and give him something new. I do my best."

In addition to being the best climber in the gym, Masato was also like a third degree black belt in karate. He was a small, quiet, polite gentleman—the opposite of Pete in a lot of ways, although they shared a good sense of humor—and I knew from some paperwork I'd seen that he was also the main investor in You So Mighty. Word around the gym was that Masato had made a ton of money at Microsoft and retired early, though he still did some kind of consulting work.

"A man of action," Pete said in admiration one time. "A warrior in the truest sense. Masato lets his life speak for him. He's too humble to discuss it, but I'd be willing to wager that he hails from a long line of Samurai. He has that sort of uncompromising nobility about him."

For the last year or so, I'd been considered the second-best climber in the gym. I could do 5.13s consistently and 5.14s occasionally, but never managed one of Pete's 5.15s. He usually had me test his new "Masato-piece" if I was around early on Buccaneer Night. So when he finished up that night, he looked at me and said, "Well?"

"Okay," I said, lacing up my shoes. By the way, my toes are pretty disgusting from all the climbing I do. Black and blue nails and stuff, from shoving them into tight cracks. Part of a climber's reality.

The route contained the usual suspects, in addition to the overhang: flexibility-testing high steps, tiny holds that required crimping of fingers and flagging of feet, underclings, gastons, sloping holds that you couldn't grab in a natural way, and several crossing maneuvers. The crux would be at the overhang, and I went for it aggressively, knowing Pete had me belayed if I missed.

I got my right hand on the small hold, swung my legs back, then used the forward momentum to lift my left foot onto a tiny edge I'd spotted parallel to my hand hold, maybe slightly above. Got it with a heel hook, and I pulled myself up with my right arm to grab another hold with my left hand.

"Jesus H. Nazareth!" Pete exclaimed.

The route got easier after that, and I topped out and read the quotation up there for the first time: *To live, to err, to fall, to triumph, to recreate life out of life.—James Joyce.*

I smiled over my shoulder as I rappelled down. Masato walked in as Pete was pummeling me on the back. At a distance you'd take Masato for a fit guy in his twenties, but up close you can see the little lines in his face and salt-and-pepper hair. He knew from Pete's reaction that I'd scaled the 5.15, and he smiled and bowed to me with his hands in the prayer position. I bowed to him, too, sort of saying, *Right back at ya.*

"Congratulations, Jordan," he added. "I knew you'd be joining me here soon." He went over to the mats, put on his shoes, stretched, did some push-ups and sit-ups, and warmed up on lesser walls. A dozen climbers were in the gym by the time he was chalked up and ready to try the 5.15.

Pete belayed him. Masato moved smoothly up the wall, looking strong. At the overhang he reached for the hold, got it, swung back, and as he went for the heel hook, he lost it. Pete took him on the rope and lowered him to the mats, seeming a little stunned.

Masato unclipped and walked over and put his arm around my shoulder. "Jordan climbed that route earlier," he announced to everyone. I was a little embarrassed, but proud, too. "Let's hear it for the best climber in the gym!" The others all clapped, and of course demanded an encore performance. And I proved it wasn't a fluke.

Pete said that Masato and I should be the first buccaneers of the evening, and we smiled at each other. Buccaneer Night is an invitation-only party. Pete jokes that no lawyers and MANY doctors are invited, although a couple of attorneys are buddies of his and regulars on Buccaneer

Night. They've promised to defend him in court if any-one sues over injuries sustained during the festivities.

While I prepared the ropes with some other guys, Pete prepared the grub. Rain or shine, he cooks salmon on a big grill out in the alley and puts a few cases of beer in ice-filled tubs. Cole slaw and macaroni salad are the other entries, all self-served on paper plates.

We tied big knots at the bottom of the ropes, for foot holds. By then the salmon was sizzling and we were ready to determine who would be the Top Buccaneer that night. This usually took about a half hour or so. Pete always wore an eye patch for the occasion and said stuff like, "Aye, matey, be lively or I'll run you through with me cutlass!"

We don't use cutlasses or other weapons, and you're not allowed to punch or kick. What you are allowed to do is swing on your rope with as much speed as you can mus-ter and bash into the other guy with your shoulders and hips. You win when your opponent falls or jumps off.

I've never lasted more than three rounds on Buc-caneer Night, despite lots of experience. We pair off by size, and I'll usually defeat other guys in the one-twenty to one-sixty pound range. Then I'll come up against a big guy, and it's all over. Bashing really favors the bigger guys, of course. It's sort of like their revenge, since smaller guys like me have a natural advantage climbing walls. We just don't have as much body to haul.

The hands-down all-time best buccaneer is Casey,

who comes in with A.J. to climb every now and then during the winter. The first time Casey showed up, Pete walked in as he was climbing a 5.4 and said, "Fetch me my pepper spray, Jordo, there's a bear on the wall!"

On his initial Buccaneer Night, Casey made the finals against Pete. They collided lightly on the first two passes. Pete used some of the tricks he'd acquired over the years—pushing off two walls before hurtling at you with double speed, and going for your hands with his shoulder, which most guys don't expect.

None of that had worked with Casey, who just shoved off the wall and swung toward Pete the third time. They were both going fast when, with a sickening thud, they met at the bottom of their respective arcs. Pete fell to the mat instantly, holding his shoulder. Casey continued swinging, then dismounted and checked on Pete with the rest of us.

"I'm okay, just need some ice," Pete said, getting to his feet. "Damn, Ragurski, I feel sorry for those poor saps across the line from you!" Pete had to ice the shoulder occasionally for three days before the swelling subsided.

Needless to say, there have been a few real fights as a result of buccaneer duels. A navy guy from the Lincoln once called Pete a "French Fruitcake" after they'd collided a couple of times, and Pete simply jumped off the rope, pointed to the door and said, "Outside!" They exchanged a few punches on the sidewalk, then came back in laughing and wiping the blood from their faces, and proceeded to get hammered together.

Anyway, Masato and I have dueled many times before, because we're about the same size. I've actually won a few bouts, but only because he can't really use any of his martial arts prowess. Plus, he goes easy on me. He's a really nice guy and I sense he doesn't want to hurt a high school kid.

This time, though, he seemed determined, maybe because I'd outclimbed him. As he swung toward me on our fourth pass his usual calm face was transformed into a mask of rage and he shouted, "Haaaa-yaaaa!"

I was so scared I jumped off the rope and ran. Everyone cracked up, including Masato. He lost a couple of rounds later and came over and said, "Sorry, Jordan. That was an unkind trick."

"No, it's cool," I said. We bowed to each other again, watched a former basketball player named Drew Andersen take Pete in the final, and then headed for the grub.

TEN

The best remedy for those who are afraid,
lonely or unhappy is to go outside, somewhere
where they can be quiet, alone with the heav-
ens, nature and God ... I firmly believe that
nature brings solace in all troubles.

—Anne Frank

On Friday, Juana asked me to come over for dinner at her house Saturday. We were sitting on the sloping grass embankment around the track, enjoying the sunshine and watching Casey and A.J. and a few others jog and stretch before practice. Only a half-dozen had qualified for the Regional Meet over the weekend.

"My parents asked me if I was serious about you when I got in the other night," she said, shoving my shoulder.

"Somebody'd kept me out a half hour past my curfew. Anyway, I said yes, you were my boyfriend and basically awesome. So they want to meet you."

I started sweating a little. "So are they going to ask me what my intentions are and all that?'

"Maybe. I told them to be cool, but you know how P-Units can be."

"Yeah, my mom is getting curious about you, too. Maybe your parents Saturday and my mom next week?"

"Deal."

I really liked it that she thought of me as her boyfriend. I'd only been a boy who was a friend to girls, before. At first I thought she might be just a wild and crazy climbing girl who happened to meet me first. And she's so hot I was sort of waiting for her to move on to some other guy. Now, I thought it might be for real.

"I should warn you," she continued. "Remember, I don't get along with my parents all that great."

"Sorry about that. I'm lucky, I get along pretty well with my mom."

"She sounds great, climbing Rainier and all that. Is she into religion?"

"Not really. She says she's a casual Buddhist. She meditates and reads books and magazines about Buddhism, but doesn't go to a temple or anything like that."

"Just a warning, my parents will invite you to join their church. They invite everybody. It's okay to say no."

"Thanks for letting me know. Do you go to church with them?"

She narrowed her eyes and shook her head quickly. "No way. They call me their little rebel, and I think I sort of remind them of themselves when they were younger."

"Did they wear tails, too?"

"No, that's my thing. I just like cats." She shrugged. "I have two, Tigger and Roo. I also have cat-shaped eyes, as you may have noticed."

"I noticed they're pretty."

She smiled. "Thanks. The other reason I wear the tail is climbing. When I'm at the gym or on a crag, I'll look down sometimes and the rope sort of looks like a tail. That's how I got the idea. Just an expression of my personality, although I get a lot of crap for it. Idiots like Briggs will step on it, pull it off. And my second day here, Mr. Knutson said I couldn't wear my tail in history class. I asked him to show me the school rule prohibiting tails, and he gave me a lecture and a referral."

"You're just a wild child," I said, tossing some grass at her. She smiled, threw some grass back at me, then turned serious.

"Can I ask you something?"

"Sure."

"Well, when you told me that your dad died, I was kind of curious. But if you don't like to talk about it ... "

"My mom doesn't like to talk about it," I said. "Most

people assume I don't either. I don't mind, really. Nobody ever asks me."

"So what happened?"

"He was on a business trip to Mexico," I said, "and he died of natural causes. That's all I know."

"Natural causes?"

"Yeah, kind of vague."

"I guess I can understand why your mom doesn't want to talk about it. Still, she must know you're curious."

"I am, but it hurts her so much if I bring it up that I've learned to just put a plug in my curiosity."

"Hmm. You're a nicer person than I am, Jordan. I'd demand some facts."

"I don't know about 'nicer.' I just can't stand to see women cry."

"Well that's some useful information," she said, and gave me a kiss.

. . .

On Saturday, I was at her house at seven sharp for the big "Meet the Parents" thing. I was thinking it would've been easier if I'd picked her up there a few times, met them casually before we did a big dinner. Too late.

Her house was a sprawling colonial, in a nice neighborhood on a bluff overlooking the Sound. I remember Mom driving us around the area at Christmas to look at the lights—the neighborhood was famous for displays that ranged from gorgeous to gaudy.

Mrs. Miller answered the door and was all smiles. She had the same perfect eyes and nose as Juana. I handed her the homemade cake Mom had insisted I bring as a gift, and she said how thoughtful and all that. In the kitchen, Juana looked a little nervous. She gave me a little hug and kiss on the cheek, and then Mr. Miller came down the stairs and shook my hand with a real firm grip. Two cats stared at me from a corner of the living room.

Juana noticed my glance and went to pick up the orange one. "This is Tigger," she said, "she's a tabby." I stroked her head—the cat's, not Juana's—and she purred. Then she brought over the other cat and introduced him as Roo. When I went to pet him, he hissed and I snatched my hand back out of range, to everyone's amusement.

"Roo's not as friendly," she said. "Should've warned you. He's a flame-point Siamese."

"Just looks like a fat white cat to me."

"Hush, Jordan, you'll hurt his feelings."

I felt a little less nervous after that. We sat down to dinner. Salad and rolls and lasagna. The Millers asked me about my family and school, and I thought I scored some points when I talked about math being my favorite subject.

"I wish Juana would take more of an interest in math," Mr. Miller said. "We have to nag her to do her homework every night."

"'Cause it's boring," she said. "No offense, Jordan. I just don't like math."

"That's okay. It's just my thing."

"Those word problems kill me."

"Do they still have the one about the two trains heading toward each other on the same track?" Mrs. Miller asked.

"Yeah, sure."

"They should make the word problems more literary," Juana said. "Then maybe I could handle them."

"A literary math problem, dear?"

"Right, like instead of trains, two knights on a quest leave the stable at the same time. They charge toward each other in a joust for the fair maiden's hand. If one is a fat knight and one a thin knight, but the thin knight is going twice as fast as the fat one, who will win?"

Everyone laughed. "Too many variables are missing," I said. "Are their lances the same length and weight? Their horses? And is the maiden fair as in average, or fair as in hot? I need more information."

Mr. Miller really liked that, and I was feeling at ease by the time Mom's dessert was served in the living room. That's when the evening fell, like Joe Simpson on Siula Grande. Smash. Bang. Cursing and broken bones.

Okay, I exaggerate, but not much. Mr. Miller started it off. "So," he said, "do you have any plans for after high school, Jordan?"

I swallowed a forkful of chocolate cake, thinking it over. "I plan to keep climbing, dirtbagging around the

West," I said, hoping they would drop it. There was a silence and they looked at each other.

"Dirtbagging?" Mrs. Miller asked.

"Yeah, that means living cheap out of your car, borrowing gear, stretching your funds to the limit," I said. "A lot of climbers dirtbag, especially in the summer."

"But how will you get funds in the first place?" Mr. Miller asked.

"Well, you know I work at the gym where Juana climbs, and the boss will let me take some time off."

"Surely you don't see working at a gym as a long-term job or career," Mrs. Miller commented.

"Mom!" Juana said.

"It's a legitimate question, dear."

I shrugged. "I'd like to make climbing a career if I could. I have some other ideas, too. More lucrative."

I can't even begin to convey how much I wanted to reel that statement back in. I'd let my ego get the best of me because I was feeling defensive about my job. Sure enough, Mr. Miller asked about my lucrative ideas.

Moment of truth. I knew Pete would've told me to have some fucking integrity and not give a damn what other people thought. So I looked at the Millers and went for it.

"Well, during the winter I plan to head to Florida and work as a second-story man."

Mr. Miller was about to shove some cake in his mouth, but he stopped with his mouth hanging open, then put down his fork. Mrs. Miller dropped hers and said, "Pardon me?"

I'm not sure why I said what I said next. Maybe I'd been hanging around Pete too much, listening to him say anything he felt like. Maybe I just wanted to see what would happen, I don't know. But I said it.

"A second-story man," I repeated. "Actually, in my case, it'll probably be a twenty- or thirty-story man. The higher up you go, the less likely you are to find a locked door."

Juana groaned and put her face in her hands. Her parents stared at me for a little while, and I guessed they weren't going to invite me to church now. Then Mr. Miller started sputtering.

"You mean a thief?" he asked. "That's your life's ambition, to be a thief?"

"No, my ambition is to be a great climber."

"But you'd steal when you weren't—what was the term? Dirtbagging?"

"It's a way to use my talents in the off-season. I don't like ice-climbing."

Wide-eyed stares. Mrs. Miller recovered first and turned to Juana. "You should have told me, dear," she said. "I would've locked up the good china."

"Mom, I didn't know," Juana said. Then she turned to me, and I could see her sort of struggling to decide whether to back me up or back off. "But I think Jordan would be good at whatever he decided to do."

Her mother's eyes narrowed a little. Juana stared right back. I was sweating like a run-down beast and wanted out of there. Thankfully, Mr. Miller changed the subject to the Everett Aquasox and their pitching staff or something like that. I was thinking about how to make an exit before they put me through more cross-examination. But there was no easy way. When he was done talking about baseball, I stood up, thanked them for dinner, said good-bye to Juana, and all but ran to my car. As I was shutting the door I heard Juana and her mom yelling at each other.

. . .

She called me on my cell a few minutes later. "Sorry about that," she said.

"No, my fault," I said. "Your folks were fine."

"No, they weren't ... I do wish you'd told me about your planned career ahead of time."

"Just never came up."

"You heading home?"

"No, I'm sort of wired. I was going to drive around for a while."

"Well, it's still early. Let's meet at school. We can chill for a while. I gotta get out of here."

. . .

On the way to Mountain View, I stopped at a convenience store. I met Juana in the school parking lot about ten minutes later. I threw my pack on and grabbed her hand, and told her I had an idea.

"I hope it's a better idea than telling my folks your lofty ambitions," she joked.

"It is," I said. "Sort of a mini-expedition."

"Okay." We walked past the Sasquatch in the dusky light and I told Juana about the side view, and she cracked up when we got to the viewing spot. "And I thought he looked shy!"

We crossed the campus to Building Six. A maple tree was in the middle of the courtyard, between the wings of the building. A heavy branch extended toward the west wing. Juana followed my gaze.

"You're not thinking of … "

"Yup, an easy climb for pros like us."

"If you say so."

"Let me lead, I've done this a few times."

The tree's lower branches required a little jump to reach. I had to put more effort than usual into it because of the heavy backpack. Then I swung my right leg onto a wide branch, pulled myself up, and sat there looking down at her. She smiled up at me with those perfect teeth and I almost fell out of the tree, she was so beautiful.

The large branch veered to the right. I had to duck under another branch, and used friction holds to climb higher. A minute later I was at a point where the branch began to taper. Part of it extended over the roof, but it was too small to hold my weight.

So I swung from the branch and grabbed the gutter at the edge of the roof with both hands. You have to watch out for gutters—some of them are really weak, but I knew from experience that this one was sturdy.

The next move was challenging because the roof had a low slope. If a roof is flat, no problem. But a slight angle means you aren't home even if you get a leg up.

I went for it hard, swinging my left leg up and doing a quick pull-up at the same time, to bring my center of gravity closer to the lip. My momentum carried me over the gutter and I scrambled quickly onto the roof.

"Ta-Da!" I said, standing up. I'd made it look pretty easy, showing off. Most climbers would have struggled with that move, probably taken three or four tries to figure it out. Most good athletes would have given up after the first attempt, and the rest of the population wouldn't have even tried.

Juana called, "I'll be right up." She handled the tree easily, then jumped and grabbed the gutter. She started swinging her legs. It was only about a ten foot drop if she fell, but she could get hurt pretty bad if she fell on her back, and that would be the case if she lost her hold while swinging up her legs. Suddenly I thought my cool idea was pretty stupid.

This was a muscle move, and while Juana was strong, she wasn't as strong as me or most guy climbers. She relied on foot placement and used her arms for balance, mostly. At the gym I'd seen her do six pull-ups warming up, which isn't bad. But me and A.J. and some of the other climbers could crank out twenty or more.

I was thinking about this when she took a deep breath, swung her right leg up and went for it. She pulled hard and her momentum was good—I thought she had it. She was wriggling, fighting for the extra inch or two that would put her on top.

I put one hand over her ankle and the other over her wrist, just an inch away, ready to grab and haul her up if she couldn't make it. Her front teeth were dug into her lower lip as she strained on the cusp. It was tough to tell which way it would go.

"Want some help?" I asked after about ten seconds, when I was sure she was going to fall. Her face was a like a Halloween mask of an angry beast, and her leg and arm muscles were trembling.

"Don't touch me!" She spat the words between clenched teeth. Not the words a guy wants to hear from his girlfriend. Maybe she wasn't as mad as she sounded, just under pressure from King Gravity.

She closed her eyes. I thought she was going to fall and was about to grab her when she roared like a lion-ess and made the crucial inches that shifted her center of gravity above the gutter. She rested there for a minute, dangling half over the edge, catching her breath.

"Face down in the gutter, I can't take you anywhere," I said to tease her. "But you did look kind of sexy when your face was all scrunched up and you were grunting."

She laughed, then crawled the rest of the way onto the roof. I was really proud of her and gave her a hug.

"Never expected to almost kill myself on a date," she said, hugging me back.

"Yeah, I was thinking it wasn't my best idea when you were hovering on the crux there."

"Hey, I made it," she said. "But next date let's go to a movie."

"Glad you still want to see me after my screw-up at your house."

"Forget it."

We smiled at each other and walked along the roof, looking at the school grounds from a bird's-eye perspective. I felt tall, like I always do on summits. We sat on the crest on the north edge of the roof and I unzipped my backpack and pulled out small seat pads and sparkling cider.

We sipped our cider and watched the setting sun light the Cascades in pink and gold while the rest of valley was in blue shadow. I put my arm around her shoulder and we snuggled close for an hour, talking, enjoying the view, kissing sometimes. I felt so happy I thought I might explode.

ELEVEN

*Fear... The right and necessary counterweights
to that courage which urges men skyward, and
which protects them from self-destruction.*

—Heinrich Harrier

The State Championship Track Meet was held in Bellevue on a Friday afternoon. Only A.J., Casey, and a miler named Joey Walker were competing, the rest of the team having been weeded out in the district and regional meets. The school cancelled the rooter bus for lack of interest and let the three guys drive down with their families rather than in a school van. Casey and Walker drove with their folks, but A.J.'s parents were coming from work, so he drove down with me and Juana.

"Hope you appreciate the sacrifice we're making here," I said. "This is a perfect day for climbing."

"My last day of track this year," A.J. said. "One more race, then I'm a full-time climber again. At least until football season."

Springtime I could handle, but I really missed A.J. in the late summer and early fall, which is the best time to climb crags. I knew football was important to him and Casey, and I tried to support them as much as I could—I'd gone to about half the games last year. I always checked the weather reports and went to games when the forecast called for rain, because I couldn't bear to miss a prime climbing day. Sometimes the forecasts were wrong, though, and I missed two killer-fine days watching football last year. A.J. knew I was dying, and on the sideline he pointed to me with his helmet, then up at the clear blue sky, and laughed in a very exaggerated way.

Today, A.J. had just broken up with his latest girl-friend, which was why he was alone in my back seat. I think she'd lasted three weeks, which was about his average.

"She wanted me to make a *commitment*," A.J. said, pronouncing the word like it tasted bad. "Can you believe that shit?"

"Yes, incredible that she'd want something so outra-geous," Juana said.

"Hey, don't get sarcastic, Medical."

"You promised not to call me that nickname anymore."

"In public, yeah," he said. "It's my private nickname for you. Medical Marijuana, that's you."

"You're going to slip up and say it around school, and then everyone will know my name."

"No way. And back to the subject, the only reason Jordo is committed to you is because your family's rich. I heard all about that house on the hill."

Juana turned to me in mock horror. "You're with me for my family's money! I thought you were after me for my humongous breasts!"

I said, "Man cannot live by breasts alone." She whacked me, but was laughing.

.   .   .

After dropping A.J. off and wishing him luck, we sat in the stands with a couple hundred other folks. A few events were going on at once, and the announcer more or less kept us informed about what to watch. Casey was up first, in the shot put and discus. He easily won the shot and finished third in the discus. Afterward, he pointed to us in the stands when he heard us clapping and whistling. His parents met him at the edge of the stands for a group hug.

"I see where he gets his size from," Juana said. "His folks are huge."

"He's always been big. I heard when he played football in grade school, parents of kids on the other teams would demand to see his birth certificate."

"To prove he was human?" Juana smiled.

"Well, he does look a little like the Sasquatch."

Walker finished fourth in the mile, and there were several other events before the hundred meter dash. I was confident A.J. would win. After watching him sprint past countless linebackers and defensive backs on his way to the end zone, it was hard for me to believe anyone was faster.

At the gun, A.J. surged to the lead. He kept accelerating away from the pack and had a good lead at sixty yards. We thought he had it won.

Gradually, though, this tall guy from Seattle Prep started closing the gap, reeling in A.J. like a fish. His feet weren't moving as fast as A.J.'s, but his strides were much longer. He drew even at ninety meters and won by a few inches.

"Can't believe it," I said.

"Too bad they don't have a fifty meter race."

Casey walked over and put his big arm around A.J.'s shoulder. The announcer said the Seattle Prep guy was a senior, so we figured A.J. would have a good shot at the title next year.

. . .

The following Wednesday in English, Mr. McGinnis

handed back our *Snow Falling on Cedars* test. Juana got a perfect score and I got an A-minus. Not bad. Probably would've had a B if I hadn't studied with her.

We were finishing the year with a poetry unit. When McGinnis had announced that the week before, I led a chorus of groans. Poetry is definitely not my thing. I don't know how I can be graded on it, either. I mean, in math you either get the problem right or you don't. There's none of this fuzzy teacher-judgment stuff.

Juana, being Miss Literature, naturally loves poetry. She was a little disappointed that I didn't share her passion for sonnets and free verse.

"Maybe you'll acquire a taste for poetry if you hang out with me long enough," she said.

"Yeah, that'll happen," I laughed. "Probably about the same time you acquire a taste for calculus."

"Hmm, good point. That's okay, it would be boring if we had everything in common."

We were already four days into the unit, and I must admit some of the poems we'd studied so far were okay. I liked the one about the athlete dying young, though some of the vocabulary was challenging. And Joy Harjo's poem about fear was awesome. At first I thought it was sort of repetitive—"I release you" and "I am not afraid" over and over again—but the second time I read it, the repetition seemed to work. The lines that really struck me were about how we give fear power.

Oh, you have choked me, but I gave you the leash.
You have gutted me, but I gave you the knife.
You have devoured me, but I laid myself across
*   the fire.*
I take myself back, fear ...

Juana and I talked about that one later. We'd both been scared so many times while climbing that it really hit home.

"Have you ever fallen?" she asked.

"Couple of times," I said. "Once I was top-roping with A.J. He was daydreaming and gave me too much rope, and I slipped and fell about five feet before he braked. A nasty adrenaline rush. The other time I was smearing my left foot and the nub under my right broke off. Lost it, but my protection held."

"I've never actually fallen," she said, "and I hope I never do. Of course, I've peeled quite a few times in the gym. I hold on as long as I can, searching for a hold, until I get sewing-machine leg. Then I call for a take."

"The fear is always there, but I've noticed that it doesn't scare me anymore," I said. "Does that make sense?"

She nodded. "I know what you mean. It's like a shadow, never far off, but you learn to smile at it after a while. I've also noticed that dealing with fear on the crags leaks into the rest of my life. You know, I'll be in a situation that could be scary, and I'll watch the fear rather than going crazy and screaming like a maniac."

.   .   .

Anyway, back to poetry. I have to admit the unit didn't suck. I definitely thought it was heading down the drain yesterday, when Mr. McGinnis announced we were going to read a story about a poet's life, along with some of his poems. I figured all male poets were real sensitive types, probably gay dudes with issues, and was planning to snooze through the reading.

So imagine my surprise when the poet, Jimmy Santiago Baca, turned out to be a former hard-core gang-banger who'd spent years in a maximum security prison. He actually credited poetry with saving his life! His free verse poems all sounded very honest, based on his experience. The one I remember best was when he was applying for early release and the parole board turned him down after he tried to read some of his poems. He compared himself to a deer and the parole board to a hunter who peered at him "through bluemetal eyes like rifle scopes."

Today, after handing back the tests, McGinnis started talking about music and poetry. "A very small percentage of poets in this country actually make a living writing poetry," he said. "But if you include songwriters as poets, the numbers go way up. I have to add, however, that good music forgives a lot of truly horrible poetry."

He had a few examples. "These are just some lyrics I've heard on the radio and jotted down over the years. Let's see.

Ah, yes. 'You and me, baby, ain't nothing but mammals, so let's do it like they do on the Discovery Channel.'"

We all laughed. "Yes, it's a touch humorous because it's so wretched. Then we have this classic line: 'I'm going to hide out under there—I just made you say underwear.' Well, move over, Keats and Shakespeare."

He pointed out that some songwriters were the real deal as poets. "The test is whether, when if you read the lyrics on the page, they hold up," he said. "Is there rhythm without the melody? Phrasing beyond the notes? Content? Imagery?" He mentioned a few of his favorites—Don Henley, Bob Dylan, Sheryl Crow, Bono, Springsteen, Sarah McLachlan.

"And then there is Leonard Cohen," he said, "who is in a league of his own. You might have heard a butchered version of his song *Hallelujah* in the first Shrek movie. Thankfully, they included the unaltered version on the soundtrack. Rufus Wainwright does a fine job with it. To me, this song speaks about how we can touch the divine through our relationships. The song is funny, sexy, even spiritual. It may mean something else to you. Great poetry is open to various interpretations."

He hit a button on his CD player. Of course, we were all listening closely for the sexy part. I thought it might have been the lines about King David watching a woman bathing on the roof and then getting a haircut from her while tied to a chair. But the real sexy part came later: *I remember when I moved in you, the holy dark was moving too, and every breath we drew was hallelujah...* Out of some reflex, Juana and I looked at each other after that line, then looked away real fast. I could feel myself blushing and guessed she was, too. Nobody seemed to be paying attention to us, and that was a relief.

Out in the hall after class, we just walked to the parking lot together, not saying much, and she told me to follow her. She drove to her house. Her parents were at work, of course, and when we got inside we kissed for a long time, and then she took me by the hand and we walked upstairs to her room. Juana locked the door, then turned to me with an expression that was sort of shy and amused at the same time, like we were in on a secret.

Which I guess we were. We'd fooled around a little, and I liked feeling her up, even if she was flat-chested. She'd stopped me when I started feeling elsewhere.

This time she didn't stop me. I was so excited that my first sexual intercourse lasted about three seconds. Juana said it was okay, and we kissed and cuddled until it was time for Round Two. Which was *much* longer—and better.

"Do you think McGinnis would give us extra credit for this?" I asked when we were holding each other after.

"Ha! I'm trying to picture my mom's face if she was reading my grades online and came to the entry, *Sex in Juana's Bedroom.*"

"So how many points would we get?"

"An infinitude, Mr. Math Man."

She got out of bed and went over to her desk. She pulled

a paper from the drawer and came back and handed it to me. "Read this," she said.

"Okay."

Climbing
By Juana Miller

High on a bold face
Climbing through space
Bloody fingers in a crack
Abyss at my back
I whisper "You're fine"
Yet look for a sign
In the distant blue
The beckoning hue
Of ridge and sky
Is this the day I die?
Head into the night
In a plunging flight?
Yes, flying is falling
Rocks below calling
Freedom and fear
Both so near
Gravitational
Inclinations
Meet
Instinctual
Destinations
And lead me ever higher

Back to the fire
The voices of friends
As the summit day ends
With tales of near woe
And smiling faces aglow.

"Hey, that's great!" I said. "You really captured the feeling."

"You think?"

"Absolutely."

She hugged me hard. "You're such a sweetie!"

I could tell the poem was important to her, but I meant it.

"I wrote that one last year," she continued, "after a climbing trip with some friends in Eugene. I have about sixty poems, and three of them have been published in magazines. When I get to a hundred, I'll weed through them, keep the best ones, and see if I can get them published as a collection. I'll publish the book myself if no one else will."

"Well, if they're all as good as this climbing one, I'll bet you find a publisher," I said, stroking her back. I was thinking about getting her flowers later, as sort of a thank-you-and-I-care-about-you gesture. And then I surprised myself a little. I said, "I love you."

She propped herself on an elbow and looked into my eyes. I was fairly sure she loved me, too, and would say so. But Juana never went for the easy line.

"About time you figured that out," she said.

TWELVE

For the ones who had a notion,
a notion deep inside, that it ain't no sin to be
glad you're alive ...

—Bruce Springsteen

On the last day of school, a half-day, A.J. suggested we go to Flowing Lake up near Monroe. I would've preferred to go somewhere alone with Juana, but she was taking off with her parents for a week-long camping vacation on Vancouver Island.

"Gonna be an awesome time," he said while eating a doughnut for breakfast. "A bunch of us are going. You should come. Have a few beers, check out the hotties, and let them check our rock-carved physiques." He gave me a little wink. "Well, mine, anyway."

"Hey, give me some credit for the beef I've been putting on," I said, flexing my biceps. He laughed. I'd put on about ten pounds of muscle in the last year, along with growing an inch or so, but my arms—like the rest of me—were still skinny. Not weak skinny, though. Lean and mean, the classic crag build.

A.J. flexed his own right arm, to show me what it was supposed to look like. A ball-shaped rock with veins. He had serious guns, along with his huge thighs and butt. "Better for football than rock climbing," he shrugged. "What can I say? This is the way I am. Might as well make the most of it."

Following tradition, when the final bell of the year rang at eleven thirty, the administration played Alice Cooper's "School's Out for Summer" over the loudspeakers. Kids were running around and everybody was smiling, including the teachers.

We took A.J.'s old Toyota to the lake. The sky was completely clear, and we were both looking at the Cascades, still snow-capped. "They're calling us," I said. "Listen: *Jordo, A.J., get your asses up here.*"

"Let's do a climbing road trip when you get back from Rainier," A.J. said. "Start with the Icicle. You keep going on about Snow Creek Wall."

"Now you're talking."

"And then head over to the Columbia River to climb

Vantage. I figure four days, the last one mostly driving back."

"Definitely. Let's say late July, before football practice starts."

"Deal. I'll tell my dad. He said I could have a couple days off for climbing here and there."

I was smiling. We had turned north off Highway 2 and gone a couple of miles toward the lake when A.J. looked down at the dashboard and mumbled, "Shit."

"What?"

"Forgot to get gas," he said. "We'll have to go back. No stations around here…though we're only about a mile out."

"Want to just risk it?" I asked. "How low are you?"

"Well, the needle says empty, but she probably has a reserve tank, right?"

"Probably."

"Screw it, let's go for it."

We were within a quarter mile when the car made a sputtering noise, stalled, crept forward a few feet, then died. A.J. pulled onto the shoulder.

"So much for the reserve tank," I said. He glared at me for a few seconds, then we both laughed.

"We can borrow some gas from the guys who're at the lake already. I have a little plastic container thing in the trunk," A.J. said.

"Okay." I started to walk toward the lake on the shoulder of the road.

"Where you going, dude?"

I turned and stared at him. "The lake, dumb shit. Like we just talked about. Then we beg somebody to take us back here and siphon some gas into your little tank."

A.J. was shaking his head. "And miss an opportunity for a great entrance?"

"What are you taking about?"

"I'm talking about pushing my car the rest of the way. Once we get over that little crest, it's slightly downhill all the way. Think about it. Think about the honeys checking out our bods. Why walk, when we can push the car and really show our muscles in action? It'll be fantastic!"

"You're nuts," I said, walking back to the car. I knew whose bod the girls would be checking out, and it wasn't mine. "Guess I'm your wingman."

"Yeah, that's the price you pay for me driving to the lake."

"Almost to the lake."

"Whatever. I'll push at the driver's door and steer, you push at the rear bumper. Let me put her in neutral." He turned the key and shifted. "Take off your shirt, Jordo. Some girls like skinny runts."

"Eat me, Muscle Brain."

He laughed and we started pushing. We were straining hard, but the car barely moved an inch. We rocked back and forth, and gradually got a little momentum, the wheels finally turning fast enough that we didn't have to kill ourselves. Hate to admit it, but A.J.'s calf muscles did look pretty impressive from my rear view, like knotted rope.

I said, "So how long are you going to be in your weight-lifting stage of development? It's a phase like puberty, right?"

"I'm gonna lift for my whole life," he said. "Look at the dinosaur legs I've got from squats. I love the weight room almost as much as a rock face and the football field, and it helps me in every sport."

"Most climbers don't lift much."

"Well, the bulk does get in the way on some faces that your skinny ass slithers over, but not often."

We were nearing the crest. Just then a car passed with a bunch of girls inside, laughing at us. To show he was brainy as well as brawny, A.J. yelled, "Hey, hotties!"

The lake came into view, sparkling in the sunshine. We did draw some attention when we started down from the ridge. We could see kids pointing at us, though we were too far away to hear what they were saying. The car was moving along at a nice clip, and we were running. Busy looking over the crowd, we didn't notice that the incline was getting steeper until the car suddenly leapt ahead.

"Oh, shit!" we both yelled. I was running as fast as I could and couldn't catch up, so I slowed down to watch. A.J. wasn't giving up that easy. He was in full sprint along-side the car, feet a blur, and he had the door handle—lost it—grabbed it again, flung it open and dove headfirst into the driver's seat. He must've hit the wheel because the car turned toward the trees and was half off the road before he got it back under control, maybe ten feet shy from a collision with Mr. Douglas Fir.

He pulled up to the crowd, braked hard, and kicked up a cloud of dust. Everyone was whooping and laughing, and he stepped out of the car and bowed, then pointed to me with a smile. What a nutcase.

As usual, he was the center of attention for the rest of the afternoon. We swam and drank some beer with the others, played some Frisbee football. We forgot all about the gas situation until people started leaving, but we didn't have to siphon—Casey had a full two-gallon metal can in his trunk for his family's lawn mower, and A.J. gave him a few bucks to borrow the contents.

There were still some girls around, and A.J., being a natural ham, still had his shirt off even though it was getting cooler and he was sweating from the activities. While pouring the gas, he rested the gas can against his stomach for support. He could have held the can with his hands but preferred to keep them on his hips, in a pose that gave the passing girls a good view of his biceps and deltoids.

Occupied as he was, he never noticed the leak in the bottom of the metal can. He never felt the warm gasoline mingle with his warm sweat and flow down his stomach. Down past his belly button. Down, down. Down to the Untanned Region beneath his shorts.

I was leaning against the hood of the Toyota sipping a soda when I noticed a curious expression on A.J.'s face. A second later the expression vanished and his face went as blank as a teacher's whiteboard in summertime.

I think a hottie was cruising by when A.J. said, "Oh, man, Jordo, my balls are on fire! My balls are on fire!"

That got everyone's attention. He noticed my soda and ran over, grabbed it, pulled out the waistband of his cutoffs and poured. The can was empty in seconds and he grabbed another off the seat of the car and repeated the process.

A couple of guys realized what was going on and brought over some water bottles. Casey started laughing so hard he fell down on the grass and rolled around like a dog, tears streaming out of his eyes. We were all laughing our asses off, but A.J. was so relieved he didn't care a bit.

He got teased pretty good afterward. In a nod to his Native American heritage, everyone was calling him Chief Balls on Fire. Nice thing about A.J., though, he could laugh at himself. Which was another reason so many people liked him.

THIRTEEN

*I like to think that a child who has seen those
stars and those mountains will ever after, surely
without ever understanding why, understand
that it is important to strive but absurd to strut.*

—Russell Baker

The night before my Rainier trip with Mom in late June, we ordered pizza to load up on carbs and checked our gear. Our two piles covered the whole living room. Mom had a checklist in her hand and went through her pile first. "Ice axe, check. Crampons, check. Headlamp, check. Three pairs of wool socks, check. Sleeping bags, check."

"Obsessive compulsive," I interrupted, "check."

"Jordan, this is important!"

"I know, I know."

Mom was really excited, and I must admit I was getting there myself. I'd never climbed a mountain over seven thousand feet, and here I was going for fourteen thousand, the toughest alpine climb in the U.S. outside of Alaska. Colorado has a bunch of fourteeners and California has a few, but Rainier is tougher because you start at five thousand feet. A lot of the other fourteeners have trailheads at around ten thousand feet. Then there are the glaciers, avalanches, and other stuff you need to worry about. Rainier is a whole different ball game.

The next morning at breakfast, Mom admitted she didn't sleep well. She went back in for a nap while I put our packs in the car and called Juana and A.J.—funny, they both said they wished they were going with us. Juana had climbed Mount Hood, and Rainier was next on her big-mountain list.

We took off about noon, heading south on I-5 through Seattle and Tacoma, then heading east for a while, then south again on a country road. It was a clear, warm day, and every now and then we'd catch a glimpse of Rainier, which of course seemed to be getting bigger as we got closer. Mom started to say "amazing" when we got a view near Ashford, but caught herself and it came out "ama..."

"I'll watch my adjectives if you keep from whining," she said. "Rainier National Park is a no whining zone."

"Tell you what, Mom," I said. "I'll give you the adjectives of your choice at the summit. But that's it. You start spouting premature adjectives, you gotta be mute at the top."

"Deal."

The trees became dense around the National Park entrance. Mom paid the fee and we drove six miles up the twisting road that runs parallel to the Nisqually River. We were booked for two nights at the National Park Inn, a sprawling old hotel with what Mom called a million-dollar view. After we checked in and got settled, she bought a wine cooler for herself and a Pepsi for me, and we sat in chairs on the Inn's front deck looking at the south side of the mountain.

I could see why people didn't usually climb the southwest side. It was all cliffs and pinnacles and hanging glaciers, from what I could see, and the ridges looked very steep. Everyone sitting on the porch was so fixated on Rainier, I was probably the only one who noticed the fine-looking cliffs about a half-mile from the hotel. They looked, in fact, a lot like Index Town Walls. I'd have to check them out sometime.

The next morning we drove back out of the park to the headquarters of Tahoma Peak Guides. "Tahoma" is the Native American name for the mountain. Most of those are better. Like "Denali," in Alaska, is so much better than "Mount McKinley." Mr. Powers mentioned that white settlers had a thing for naming mountains and other landmarks after themselves or their buddies, whereas the

Natives named them after spirits and things like that. Zenny would've said that was better karma.

Anyway, the TPG headquarters was a cool place, with bouldering and climbing walls, gift and rental shops, and a café. We found a picnic table with our names on it and met the other folks in our group. Patrick and Linda were a married couple in their thirties from Los Angeles, and Tony and Rod were a couple of retired Coast Guard officers in their mid-fifties. Tony was about my height and fit looking, while Rod was about six-three and had a belly. I would've guessed him at about two-forty, which was a lot of weight to carry up a mountain along with a heavy pack.

The guides came out of a meeting about twenty minutes later. They introduced themselves and told us about their experience guiding and climbing. They'd both done Rainier like forty times or so.

Other than that, they were opposites in every way. Candice was from Montana, a very hot skier-climber-runner type, a couple of inches over five feet, maybe, and totally muscular even in her face. If Juana were around she would've been totally pissed at the way I gawked. Evan was a tall guy from Bellingham with a wispy beard and a crooked-toothed smile. He had wide shoulders, but the rest of him was thin as spaghetti. And while Candice seemed sort of loud and outgoing, he was quiet and seemed kinda shy.

They went over equipment and looked over what we

brought. We were all prepared, which seemed to relieve them. We hauled our stuff over to a bus and drove back into the park, winding up the road to Paradise, a parking area at five thousand feet with a visitor's center, hiking trails, and alpine views to die for. I could tell Mom wanted to drop a string of adjectives at Paradise, but she settled for looking around with a smile.

The first day was all training and evaluation. They wanted to teach us a few things and check our fitness. Right off they mentioned the sun—we needed protection with clothing, sunglasses, lip balm, and sun block. "A key word," Evan said, "is *re-apply*. The sun reflects off the snow and glaciers up here and you can get a bad burn if you're not careful."

We hiked about an hour to a snowfield with a lot of rolling hills, where they went over ice-axe instruction. Basically, if you're falling, you dig the pick of the axe into the snow and stop yourself—they called it a "self-arrest," which sounded funny. They said you'd also arrest if you were roped up and someone on your team fell.

The first couple of times, Mom swung her axe like she was chopping a tree. "Angie, you want to keep the axe close to your shoulder," Candice said. "You're much stronger there, and you could easily lose your axe swinging it out like that."

We practiced by sliding down a steep hill in various positions. Evan and Candice wanted to get us in the habit of being alert to our teammates, so we had to yell

"Falling!" as we started sliding. When it was Rod's turn, instead of "Falling" he yelled "Fumble!"

"Fumble?" Candice asked after he'd stopped sliding.

"Sorry," he said, dusting snow off as he trudged back to the group. "Reminded me of a football drill I did as a kid. Old habits die hard, I guess."

After another hour of practicing, we took a lunch break. I was sitting on my pack next to Evan, and mentioned that the self-arrest drills were fun. "They are," he said, "but keep in mind that this is serious, too. I saw an axe used for real a few years ago. I was climbing with a buddy in the northern Cascades, and he fell."

I noticed that everyone had stopped eating and was listening. "I was below him," Evan continued, "kicking into the steps we made on the way up. I saw a flash to my left. That's how fast it was. He went flying by me, and at that speed he would've died or been severely injured if he'd hit the rocks below us."

"What happened?" Patrick asked.

Evan swiveled his eyes toward him. I noticed they were very tough blue eyes now, not shy like before. "He knew how to self-arrest. He rolled over on his belly and planted his axe. It didn't catch the first time, but he was determined and finally got it planted and arrested himself. That's one thing I wanted to emphasize. Technique is important, but the main thing is to be aggressive and get yourself stopped. My friend stopped himself about twenty feet short of the rocks."

"Geez," Tony said.

"Yeah, it was intense. He had a badly sprained ankle and had to limp about four miles to the trailhead, but that beats dying or breaking a leg."

We all nodded, understanding the importance of what they were teaching us now. After lunch, we put on the harnesses we would use on our rope teams. Candice and Evan were helping the Coast Guard guys, and Mom strapped hers on with surprising ease. Linda and Patrick were struggling, so I helped them after securing mine. When I looked up, Evan and Candice were smiling at me.

"Obviously you have some experience," Candice said.

"Yeah, I teach a belay class at the gym where I work."

"Told you he looked like a climber," Evan said. "Good to know."

For the next couple of hours they taught us how to walk on rope teams and use the rest step and pressure breath to cope with the altitude. Then we packed up and headed down to Paradise. Evan walked up alongside me. "Jordan," he said quietly, "your experience and fitness make you a key member of this group. We're going to depend on you. My only criticism is that you're not resting on your rest step. Way too quick, buddy. Remember that you're part of the team and we have to all keep the same pace, even if you're capable of going much faster."

"Okay." I nodded. "I'll focus on that tomorrow."

"Right on."

. . .

Mom was a little tired from the training day and took a nap before dinner while I sat on the deck and read Joe Simpson's *Touching the Void*. I'd seen the docudrama and had been meaning to read the book, and the additional details made it a page-turner even though I already knew the basic story. Every now and then I'd put the book down and look up at Rainier. Some clouds had moved in and covered the summit, but I could still see plenty of rocks and glaciers. *Tomorrow*, I said to myself. *I am gonna climb you tomorrow.*

The next morning was a little misty, and I was worried our window of good weather was closing. At TPG, though, Candice said the report was good. "This stuff is going to burn off."

We boarded the bus for Paradise again. Mom said she was feeling strong.

We followed the Paradise Trail from the parking lot, crowded with a combination of climbers and tourists taking day hikes, many of them in T-shirts and flip-flops. "Some of them get carried away," Linda said. "Swear to god, I saw a guy on a glacier wearing tennis shoes and a day pack, no ice axe or partner, and clueless that he was standing over a crevasse."

The day was perfect, warm but with a nice breeze off the glaciers, and the summit seemed to be calling me. Camp Muir was our destination for the afternoon, and

Candice and Evan said it was about a five-hour hike up the snowfield. We used trekking poles and kept our ice axes strapped to our packs.

The guides switched off leading and bringing up the rear. Both had to remind me to slow my pace, which was tough but I got the hang of it after the first break. We took a fifteen-minute break every hour. We were all together the first two breaks, but then Rod's weight began to tell, and he fell back.

Even I was a little tired and thirsty when we stopped for the final break. I saw exhaustion on Mom's face for a second, but then she smiled and gave me a thumbs up. We sat on our packs and looked back at the rolling blue ridges to the south. Mount Adams, another volcano about twelve thousand feet high, looked deceptively close. I was surprised we could see Mount Hood in the distance, all the way down in Oregon, and the sooty slopes of St. Helen's to the southwest.

We sipped water and ate candy bars and power bars, and put on more sun block. Then a sudden roar sounded, like a jet taking off, and we looked up to see a cloud of dust and tumbling boulders. Some were the size of minivans and rolled as far down the snowfield as we were, although they were about a half-mile to the west. Still, everyone got very quiet.

To lighten the mood, Patrick began teasing Linda. "You're really sweating, honey," he said. "It's pouring off you like a river."

"Women don't sweat," Linda replied. "We glow. Isn't that right, Angie?"

"Absolutely," Mom said.

"Well, you're glowing like a pig," Patrick said, and we all laughed. Linda threw a cheese stick at him.

"If you look up the slope, you can see Camp Muir," Candice said, pointing. It looked like it was a couple hundred yards away at most. "Distances are deceptive up here, as you might've noticed. We're about a half hour out."

"How you doing, Rod?" Tony asked when his friend reached the group. He held up a hand—he was panting—and collapsed on his pack. Mom and I looked at each other, wondering the same thing. After a minute he started breathing easier.

"I'm okay," he said, turning to look at Tony. He didn't say anything else, just got out his sun block, food and water.

"Five minutes," Candice said. Rod, who had barely been sitting two minutes, let out a little groan. Evan added, quietly, "Not for you, buddy. Take all the time you need. I'll climb with you the rest of the way."

Candice was right—the rest of the way to Camp Muir was longer than expected. We got there about four o'clock on the dot and put our stuff in the hut. It was two levels, pretty rustic, with an outhouse behind it on the north side. That was no big deal, it was just like a lot of campgrounds, but I saw Linda wincing in disgust after exiting. Guess they stayed in motels down in California.

By the time we were settled, Evan and Rod arrived. Rod was pale and breathing hard. He sat inside the hut for about five minutes just sipping water and generally recovering. Candice came over to talk to him.

"You okay?"

"Middling," he said. "My hamstrings and calves are cramping a little, and I'm getting back spasms."

I was half listening, and watching from my upper bunk. Her facial expression wasn't sympathetic but it wasn't critical, either. Just totally neutral, working the problem.

"Your pace is slower than we use up here," she said. "I'm concerned that you could slow down your rope team. And if Evan has to go back with you, he'd have to take another member of the group, just because we couldn't have one guide and a massive rope team."

Head down, Rod nodded.

"The cramps are a problem, too," she added. "We're going to be climbing again in about seven or eight hours. Higher altitude, of course, and steeper terrain in parts."

He absorbed this, then he looked her in the eye. "I've reached my high point," he said. "I don't want to take the summit away from anyone else. My pace is pretty glacial compared to the rest of you."

She gave him a quick smile and said she respected his honest assessment. He'd stay at Camp Muir while the rest of us went for the summit. Word spread fast and everyone felt bad for him.

Mom was pretty wiped, too, but she was able to keep the pace and was recovering fast. We poured hot water in our ready-to-eat meal packets—I had chicken alfredo—and let them sit after stirring.

"Don't worry about trying to sleep," Evan told us while we waited. "Rest is the main thing. We leave the sleeping bags and extra food here, so your packs will be lighter. Get off your feet, stretch out and rest. We'll let you know the situation between eleven and three. Based on the fine weather, things are looking good."

We'd climb at night because the cold night air keeps the snow bridges on the glacier firm. They get slushy and might have broken if we'd started at a reasonable hour and came back across them in the afternoon.

No one could sleep, at least not until around eight or nine, and sort of fitfully then. I finally fell asleep around ten and it seemed like five minutes later that Candice came in and flipped on the lights. I was surprised that my watch read five after twelve. "It's a beautiful night," she said. "Let's go climb Mount Rainier!"

There was sort of a groggy cheer and we all started getting packed up. The guides encouraged us to eat and use the outhouse. "We stay roped up the whole time," Candice said, "so there's zero privacy. We haul down EVERYTHING with us, including excrement." She held up a blue bag for emphasis. I went straight to the outhouse and shit like my life depended on it.

It took us about an hour to get ready. Headlamps,

crampons, ice axes—all that stuff we'd been lugging around was finally getting used. I was on the back of Candice's rope team, with Mom and Tony in the middle. Evan, Linda, and Patrick were on the other. Rod, standing at the door, looked sad as he waved and wished us luck.

Getting ready in the dark, I hadn't really had time to look around. Now, as we traversed north across Cowlitz Glacier, I noticed the stars. Rivers and islands of stars in the blue-black sky, brighter and more numerous than I'd ever seen before. When we reached the rocks of Cadaver Gap on the far side—the name creeped Mom out—I looked back and saw the headlamps of other teams that were on the glacier, flickering beneath the looming mass. Something about the scene just hit me. It was so powerful and beautiful that, swear to god, I almost started crying, and I'm not a crying kind of guy.

I pulled myself together and we crossed the Gap. Next we had to cross Ingraham Glacier to Disappointment Cleaver. Another traverse dominated by the sharp, triangular outline of Little Tahoma Peak on our right. We took a break on the rocks of Disappointment Cleaver. "Good job, everyone," Candice said. "Sit down, put on another layer, eat and drink."

"Okay, where's the Starbucks?" Patrick joked.

"How you doing, Mom?" I asked.

"So far, so good," she said. "But that was just a traverse. The big climb is coming up."

It came quick. We did a steep section on the Cleaver, and then, as the sky lightened in the east, we started up Emmons Glacier. For the first time I really felt the altitude and understood the importance of the rest step. Now it seemed more natural, rather than something I had to keep reminding myself to use.

I could tell Mom was tired, but she never stopped moving. We fell into a slow rhythm—step, rest on straight back leg, step, rest again. A pressure breath every now and then to clear the lungs. It would've been boring except that we were on top of a glacier with hidden crevasses and surrounded by sheer rock walls, sublime and scary at the same time. All that kept it interesting for me.

With the sun rising at our backs, we kept pushing, and then Candice turned and said, "We're at the crater rim." I was watching Mom and my steps, and hadn't noticed that we'd made it—the tough part, anyway. The true summit was still about forty minutes away, on the other side of the crater.

We rested awhile, then plodded through the alpenglow to our destination. We all laughed and hugged and took pictures.

"Well?" I asked Mom as we looked around at the new day from the top of the Pacific Northwest.

"Stupendous!" she said. I waited for more, but she shook her head. "Words don't do this place justice." A moment later we were all shocked to see a red butterfly fluttering along, vivid against the white vistas.

"We see them up here sometimes," Candice said. "They get caught in wind currents—or maybe just get lost."

Evan reminded us that most accidents happen on the way down, and then we started back to Camp Muir. Now that the sun was out we could get a better idea of what we'd climbed. During a break, Candice pointed to a crevasse that looked like a monster's gaping mouth. "That's another reason we take you up in the dark," she joked. "A lot of folks wouldn't keep walking if they saw that."

Back at Muir, we rested and ate lunch, then packed up and headed down to Paradise. It had taken us five hours to get up to Muir, but less than half that to get down. Still, everyone was tired, and it was nice to glissade—a fancy French word for sliding on your ass down a mountain.

Because of his size, Rod was the best glissader, creating a chute like a toboggan that the rest of us gratefully used. We could tell he was disappointed not to summit himself, but he seemed to be rallying. "If you think about it," he said while munching on a granola bar during our last break, "I saved all your lives."

We stared at him. "Gotta explain that one, buddy," Tony said.

"Well, you're all a bunch of little runner types, Tinkerbelling your way across the glaciers to the summit. If I was roped to you, I'd be walking along like Frankenstein—clomp, clomp, clomp—and probably would've broken through a snowbridge, dragging you all with me into an icy tomb."

Nervous laughs, because while his scenario was meant to be funny, we'd all seen a few of those scary crevasses. "I'll buy you a beer for not coming with us," Tony joked.

"Hell," Linda said, "I'll buy you a pitcher."

. . .

Back at TPG headquarters, there was some lag time while folks used the rest rooms and returned rental gear. I was sipping a Coke at the table in the café where we were going to have a celebration when Evan walked over and sat down.

"You did a helluva job, Jordan. It was a pleasure to climb with you."

"Thanks, Evan. It was much cooler than I was expecting."

"I get that reaction from a lot of kids your age. You know, you ought to try out to be a guide in the next couple of years."

"Yeah?" I instantly liked the idea.

"Sure, get some more experience on big mountains, take our course on crevasse rescue, and keep doing your thing at the climbing gym and on the crags. You were very patient helping Linda and Patrick with their harnesses, and that's an attribute that many great climbers simply don't have. We look for folks with solid skills, athleticism, and teaching ability."

"This would be a great summer job."

"The best. But keep in mind that it's very competitive. Might take you a few years before you make the team." With a wink he added, "Maybe a few years down the road would be best. We don't care, but some of our clients might be freaked out being led by a guy who looks like he's fifteen."

I laughed, and he added, "Got two words for you, Jordan, that will help you get out of your teens faster than anything else: facial hair. Get some facial hair, buddy."

FOURTEEN

*The hardest battle you're ever going to fight is
the battle to be just you.*

—Leo Buscaglia

The next few weeks were regular summer stuff. I
worked at the gym, hit the crags a few times, made
fireworks with Juana on the Fourth of July, and told
everyone about the Rainier trip and maybe trying out
as a guide. Juana and I hung out as much as possible,
although not as much as I would've liked because of our
work schedules. She was putting in long hours waitress-

ing at a fish house at the marina—and making me a little jealous talking about all the guys who hit on her.

Remembering Evan's advice about getting more alpine experience, I made plans to climb Glacier Peak—a ten-thousand footer north of Highway 2—over Labor Day weekend, and Juana said she'd love to go with me. I would've liked A.J. there, too, but he'd be in football mode then.

A.J. and I were excited about our climbing trip to the Icicle and Vantage. Juana was hoping to join us for the first day, then drive back in her car the next morning.

The Friday night before, I had to work. I was behind the counter with Pete, looking over inventory lists, when a smiling man walked in. Pete introduced himself and they started chatting while I went to a nearby chair to put on my climbing shoes.

Turned out the guy Pete was talking to was a minister at the Lutheran church a couple of blocks down. He was trying to get a good gym deal for the kids in his church and, after a little negotiating, Pete gave him one.

I smiled a little listening to them, because Pete inserted his usual "fucks" and "shits" into the conversation. The minister looked slightly taken aback, maybe thinking Pete could use some religion. He invited him to attend services.

"No thanks, I'm not a churchgoer," Pete said pleasantly. "But I do have great admiration for Martin Luther."

"That's encouraging," the minister smiled. "So do I, of course."

"Hell yes," Pete continued. "Martin Luther could drink copious quantities of beer and boasted that he could drive the devil away with a single fart. Talk about reaping what you sow."

"Well, I never heard that," the minister said. "He was a scholar…"

"And he was banging nuns!" Pete exclaimed. "Jesus, I love it!"

"Uh, I don't believe that's accurate…"

"Sure it is. He married a nun, didn't he?"

"A former nun, a woman escaping the repressive church…"

"A bride of Christ nonetheless, and you think she was Luther's first? I mean, no wonder he was opposed to worshiping Mary as an icon—he probably would've taken a shot at her, too."

"That's preposterous!"

"No more so than Luther. Let's not forget that he advocated the murder of uprising peasants and was a vicious anti-Semite—but as you said, he was a scholar as well. A man of parts. Still, even with the Reformation, Lutheranism is too close to Catholicism for my taste. I've heard that the primary difference is that Lutherans sing all the verses."

The minister staggered out the door, spluttering and steaming. "Well, another customer I've lost with my big mouth," Pete said with a smile. "I should let you handle the public relations side, Jordo."

. . .

Juana came into the gym after work, looking beat. She did a 5.4 to warm-up, then a 5.7, but just sat on the mats and stretched a little after that.

"You ready for the Icicle?" I asked.

"Hopefully."

"What do you mean?"

"My parents are freaking," she said. "I put off telling them, and they didn't buy that A.J. would be our chaperone."

I knew why they wouldn't buy it. A couple days after Juana had returned from the vacation with her folks, Mrs. Miller had come home early and caught me coming out of Juana's bedroom, pulling on my shirt and zipping my jeans. I was totally embarrassed.

She yelled at Juana—who yelled back—and then told me to get out. She called my mom, who tried to be upset, but I think she was more surprised than anything. She gave me a lecture that night about being a man, taking responsibility, not using women for sex, that sort of thing. I told her I loved Juana, and after she picked herself up off the floor, she was totally cool.

"So you'll know later tonight if you can go?" I asked Juana.

"Yeah, that's when the verdict comes down. I'm not

sure if they're more upset because they know we've been sleeping together or because of your future career as a thief."

"Thought that was old news."

"Not in my house. How did your mom take it when you told her?"

"Uh, well, I only sort of told her."

Her amber eyes narrowed a little. "So you haven't actually told her?"

"Not really."

"But you felt free to share that particular career plan with my folks?"

"They asked." I shrugged.

"Well, I liked that you were honest with them, but don't you think you should be honest with everyone?"

I was thinking about arguing that, but she was right. Not saying much to my mom was still kind of a lie. She hadn't asked lately because I had good grades, and I'd assured her freshman year that I was just joking when I mentioned second-story stuff.

"Yeah, you're right," I said.

"Fine, but it's a little late to concede the point. Geez, Jordan, you knew my folks would react like they found an eyeball in the lasagna, right?"

"I was more focused on being up front about who I am than their reaction."

She nodded. "Fair enough. I like to be up front myself, so I can't really criticize you, can I?"

"I feel a 'but' in there."

"You wish you could feel my butt," she said with a smile, lightening the mood.

"True." I laughed. "As Pete would say, you have an exquisite ass."

"Why thank you. To get back to the topic, though, are you really serious about being a part-time thief?"

"Yeah," I shrugged. "I think it'd be fun."

"Fun?" she asked, then shook her head. "I thought you were a realist."

"I am. What do you mean?"

"I mean, I think your plan to be a second-story man is bullshit you say to shock adults and impress your friends."

I was really hurt that she'd say that. Pete was the only friend I'd told. I might've told A.J., but information wasn't safe with him because he liked to talk about everything with everyone. I didn't want word of my illicit career spreading around school and getting me in trouble—again.

"I can tell you're mad," Juana continued, "but as a climber you can handle hard truths and cold reality, right?"

"Yeah, I can. And I plan to be a second-story man during the off-season. That's the truth. Just 'cause it bothers you doesn't mean you have to put me down."

"I'm not putting you down. I'm criticizing your career plan."

"Not much difference."

"Yes, there is. You like the idea of climbing buildings and stealing from the rich—or how did you put it when we talked about it before? 'Equitable redistribution of wealth'? That might be true, but it's not the whole truth."

"Oh, and you know what my whole truth is?"

"Yeah. And so do you. The truth is, if you really did your high-rise act, eventually you'd be caught."

"Maybe, maybe not."

"I thought you were Mr. Realist?"

"I am!"

"Then admit you'd eventually be caught!"

"I said MAYBE I would!" Some climbers on the nearby walls turned and stared. We were both too focused and angry to care.

"No maybe about it. You're a numbers guy, so you know, statistically, that you'd be caught sometime."

"What is statistically true is not necessarily true in individual experience."

"Yeah, that's a realistic attitude."

"Whatever," I said.

"Don't blow me off with 'whatever.' You'd be caught and sent to prison. And then what happens to your relationships? Your job prospects? Your body?"

I stared at her. "My body?"

She stared back. "You really haven't thought this through."

"About going to prison? No, that's negative thinking. I don't think through falling off faces, either."

"But you do everything you can to avoid falling off faces, whereas if you start breaking into condos in Miami Beach, you'll eventually be in prison. Don't be in denial."

Had to admit her logic was pretty solid, but I didn't admit it out loud because I was pissed. "*Whereas*?" I asked instead. "God, you're already little Miss English Teacher."

"Little Miss English Teacher will be writing great poetry and climbing fantastic walls during the summer, while you'll be in a cell with a guy who, statistically speaking, will be a lot bigger than you."

I didn't like where she was headed. "I can take care of myself."

The eye roll again, followed by her deep-voiced impression of a scary guy. "'Why don't you scooch over here and cuddle with Bubba, little fella.'"

"Sick!"

"That's your reality," Juana said.

"Well, my reality this weekend is I don't feel like climbing with you, so don't worry about talking to your folks."

She looked hurt for a second. I felt angry, then mean, then sorry. But not sorry enough to apologize.

"Fine," she said, and walked out of the gym.

FIFTEEN

For a man's reach must exceed his grasp,
else what's a heaven for?

—Robert Browning

The Icicle is exactly a hundred miles east of Everett, so you'd figure it would take maybe ninety minutes to drive there on the highway. The problem is that Route 2 is twisty, hilly, and slow as a result of all the little towns in the western foothills of the Cascades—Monroe, Sultan, and a few others with stoplights. And with only a single lane in each direction, it gets super crowded on summer weekends, especially Sunday afternoons heading back west. A few times, the drive back from the Icicle has taken me five hours.

We were up at five and on the road at six, me driving, and both of us pretty quiet while we sipped coffee and slowly came awake. I was thinking about Juana, of course, and was bummed that she wasn't with us. I kept replaying our fight and felt an ache—an actual physical pain—in my gut. I wanted to talk to her, but part of me was still a little mad.

Just a few patches of snow remained on the ski slopes at Stevens Pass, right around four thousand feet. As soon as we started heading downhill on the eastern slope, the hills changed from lush green slopes with a little rock to rocky dry slopes with a little green.

Storms off the Pacific typically dump their wad on the west side of the Cascades and run out of energy after the passes, leaving the east side clear and dry. Climbers in Leavenworth—the town near the Icicle, which is what everyone calls the canyon with great walls—seem happier than those on the west side, and I'm pretty sure the sunshine has a lot to do with it. I'd climbed the Icicle about a dozen times over the last few years, mostly with A.J., so I knew the place fairly well.

"So here's the plan," I said.

"I'm all ears," A.J. said. "Actually, that's you, isn't it?"

"Ha, ha."

"Just yanking your chain, Jordo. What's the plan?"

"Okay, you become a football stud at U-Dub, then go pro."

"Good plan so far."

"Yeah, and you make a few million bucks and retire at twenty-seven before you get the shit completely beat out of you."

"Okay."

"Meanwhile, I take the money you loan me—note the word LOAN—and open a climbing shop or guide service in Leavenworth. Maybe a combo. The business starts turning a profit, I start paying back the loan. And then when you retire you move here and we become partners."

He was nodding. "Not a bad plan, dude. I like it. We could call the place 'A.J.'s.'"

"I was thinking, 'Jordo's.'"

We talked names for the next ten miles, and considered Peak-a-Boys, Summit Samurais, Mountain Masters, Wall Toppers, Face Kings, Crag Scalers, and various combos. We finally settled on Crag Masters Guide Service. "We could add 'and mountaineering shop' if we go in that direction," A.J. said.

"Works for me."

We made good time and turned onto Icicle Road a little after eight. We generally tried to avoid Leavenworth, which is usually crowded with tourists and has a fake Bavarian-village feel. "Kitschy" was the word Pete used to describe the place.

We'd been to the Icicle in April, for two days over spring break, and had been anxious to get back ever since. A mile or so down we stopped at a shop for more coffee and a couple of muffins, and water and sandwiches for later.

Sipping our beverages in the parking lot, we leaned against my old Dodge Neon and looked at the small mountains to the south and west. They were dry, like I said before, but there'd been a few major fires over the years, and entire hillsides were burns—raw stumps, small trees and shrubs, and barren rock.

Below the brown peaks, Icicle Creek thunders down the canyon, making hearing on the crags tough sometimes. The creek is popular with rafters and kayakers, who are almost as crazy as climbers, and skiers love the area in winter. We both liked the idea of living in a place with a bunch of other crazy X-Sport jocks.

We finished our coffee and were driving farther into the canyon when A.J. spotted Alison Weaver on a trail above the road. She's a climber and guide we'd met on the crags out here. I pulled over.

"Hey, Alison!" A.J. yelled. She was walking along the rocky trail in flip-flops and holding a cup of coffee, a client in front of her. I could tell he was a client because he was already wearing his helmet and was too fat to be an actual climber. She told him to keep going up the trail, she'd be along.

"Hi A.J., Jordan. How're you guys?"

"Just waking up. We're going for Snow Creek."

"Big time. Have fun."

"What are you up to?"

"Just got back from Denali. We were stuck at fourteen for five days, but we did eventually summit. I'm wiped, but I have a client." She said it nice, because he was tripping along the trail within earshot, but rolled her eyes to make her point. We tried not to laugh. She was taking him to an easy crag with a low angle and a bunch of good cracks and holds.

"Have fun yourself," A.J. said.

She snorted a smile and continued up the trail, and we headed up the road. We noted that she looked even thinner than usual, and her face was a little raw from all the wind and high-altitude sun. "Guess that'll happen if you're stuck at fourteen thousand feet in a storm," A.J. said. "Most girls I know wouldn't go anywhere they couldn't use make-up and a hair dryer."

"Yeah, that's another thing I like about Juana."

"I knew you were thinking about Medical." He smiled. "She reminded me of Alison the first time I met her. Don't worry, dude, she's crazy about you. You'll work it out."

"Hope so."

"Trust me, I know girls," he said. "In fact, I'm guessing she'll probably marry into our partnership." He shoved my shoulder and laughed. "Admit it, Jordo, you want to marry Juana."

"I want to marry Juana," I repeated. "Makes me sound like a druggie with bad grammar."

We both laughed, but I must admit he was reading my mail. I'd been thinking about what life would be like with Juana, and until our fight it all looked like peaks and roses.

"The client part of the business would be the toughest," I said to change the subject. "Gotta put up with the fat and the rich."

"Yeah, but you and your mom were just clients on Rainier, and you're good folks, so most of 'em are probably okay. They will be less rich when we're through with 'em. I don't mind the rich, seeing as I plan to be that way myself, but if I ever get arrogant about the money just shoot me, dude. I hate those jerks."

"I'm sure we'll have to deal with a few of that kind. Remember when Alison was telling us about Aconcagua in April? Being stuck in a tent for three days last winter with a pair of asshole clients?"

"Every job has a downside, I guess," he said. "I love playing football, but getting nailed by guys as big as Casey is a definite downside."

. . .

The trailhead to Snow Creek Wall is about four miles from Highway 2. One other car was in the lot when we arrived. We unloaded our packs, filled out the trail permit, and started walking. The two-mile hike would have us all warmed up by the time we reached the base. After about a mile I saw movement out of the corner of my eye, at the same time that A.J. yelled, "Snake!" The rattler slithered off the sunny top of a rock and, to our relief, headed away from us.

"The wall isn't the only scary thing around here," I said.

Snow Creek would be the biggest wall we'd ever climbed, about eight hundred feet. It ranges from 5.6 to 5.12 in difficulty. We decided to climb a route called Outer Space, highly rated and challenging. Probably take us seven or eight pitches and most of the day to reach the top.

We both stopped on the trail when we cleared the last switchback and looked up at the mountain. "Holy shit!" A.J. said. "Look at that wall!"

"A beauty."

"Yeah, a BIG beauty."

"Perfect for the first day of a road trip."

We put down our packs, put on our climbing shoes, and started to prepare our harnesses, helmets, rope, and protection.

"How about if I lead the first pitch," A.J. said, "and you take the second, and we leapfrog like that the rest of the way?"

"Fine by me."

We stashed our big packs in a crevice and covered them with a rock, hoping to keep varmints out. We double-checked all the gear, put on some sun block, and looked over the wall above us. Then we tied into the rope and he started up.

The first pitch was nothing special, with good holds the whole way, and A.J. moved quickly, pausing only to place protection, while I fed out the rope. When he reached the end of the pitch, he yelled, "Your turn!"

"On belay?"

"Belay on, dude."

"Climbing." I started up, moving smoothly, removing the protection A.J. had placed, smiling all the while. I'm happiest when I'm moving up some wall and working the problem. Pure fucking joy, as Pete would put it.

I reached the belay ledge and sat next to him. "One down," he said.

I led the next pitch. Started easy, but about twenty feet up the holds became small and I needed to crimp onto them with my fingers. I signaled A.J. when I had the anchor built, and he started up while I belayed him. As usual he was moving too fast. He was always a better climber when he led and didn't have anyone to compete against. He stopped abruptly when he came to the small holds, and I could hear him cussing.

His feet were well-positioned, but he couldn't seem to find anything with his hands. Finally he found a way, a bit to the left of the route, and continued up until he was next to me.

It's a matter of pride and style to stay on route, not to mention safety—if you go too far to the left or right, you swing like a pendulum if you fall and can get banged around.

"Shithead," A.J. said when he reached the ledge.

"Asswipe," I smiled back. We both knew he was mad at himself.

"I couldn't find anything."

"They were small but solid. Your hands are too messed up." Partly I was trying to give him an out, although he does have a couple of badly gnarled fingers from football. Mostly he just doesn't have confidence crimping onto small holds.

The next pitch took A.J. up to Two Tree Ledge, which involved a tricky traverse. He did a great job with it.

"Nice!" I said after joining him on the big ledge.

"Yeah, a comeback," he said. We looked over the valley while resting and drinking some water, eating candy bars. A.J. took some pictures and I flicked away a few ticks.

My turn. The fourth pitch was tough at the start. I was moving slowly. After fifteen feet or so it got easier, until I came to the crux finger traverse. It was about fifteen feet across. I put in a lot of protection and had to work slowly, and my arms were wiped out by the time I reached the belay ledge and built an anchor.

A.J. handled it with surprising ease. His upper body strength comes in handy on some crags, no doubt, though Juana was right that he relied on it too much. The next couple of pitches were pure fun—a three-hundred foot hand crack, the best in the state, and we leapfrogged it until we were at Library Ledge.

I led the final pitch. The crack ran out about fifteen feet from the top. There were good chicken head holds, but the first one was just a little above my reach. I was on my tiptoes, stretched out as far as I could go, touching it but not able to grip it. Then I saw a foothold I could use to get the final inches. Don't know how I missed seeing the thing—I must've been a little tired.

The rest of the chicken head holds were within easy range, and soon I was standing at the top. Other than Rainier, it was the most satisfying climb I'd ever made. When A.J. joined me a few minutes later, he grabbed me in a hug that almost crushed me. Then his eyes went wide.

"Bears!" he yelled.

I about jumped off the mountain. I turned and saw a few mountain goats sitting on a patch of snow. A.J. realized he'd mixed up his mammals and we started laughing at the same time.

"Dude, you must be really wasted," I said.

"Must be," he agreed. "But they're about the same size as a black bear."

"Yeah, but bears are dark, right? Hence the name 'black' bear? And they really don't look much like goats. You gotta get your eyes checked, A.J."

"You're never gonna let me forget this one, are you, Jordo?"

"No, probably not."

We sat down and ate a late lunch, debating whether to throw some scraps to the "bears." The usual rule of thumb is not to feed any animals in the wild, so we didn't. We packed up and started down the descent trail, and it included a lot of steep, rocky gullies, so we had to be careful. We met a couple of other climbers near the base—Mike and Brian, brothers from Spokane, also heading out. They'd completed a different route, Hyperspace. We found our packs unmolested and headed down the trail with them, chatting but also keeping an eye out for snakes.

We were pretty wiped by the time we got back to my car. Brian and Mike suggested we camp with them at Eightmile Campground, and we told them we'd planned to head there anyway. They already had their tent set up and told us the site number. They were going into town to get some food and beer, and we gave them some bucks and a short list. Ordinarily you wouldn't hand money over to dudes you met less than an hour before, but they seemed like good guys and we both tended to trust other climbers.

We drove deeper into the canyon, to the campground, and set up our tent next to the site of our new friends. We had time for a little nap before they showed up. We got the fire going and had burgers, baked beans, potato salad, and cookies, along with a few beers each—well, I only had two, my limit after the Index debacle. A.J. told them the whole story, and they teased me about being a light-weight high school guy. Had to admit it was true.

We sat around the fire talking about climbing and girls, laughing at everything, until after midnight. A.J. was smiling when he ducked into the tent. I remember that, and the wonderful day.

SIXTEEN

*You paid some way for
everything that was any good.*

—Ernest Hemingway

The next morning, I cooked bacon and eggs in the
frying pan I'd brought. Used everything, cooking
breakfast for Mike and Brian, too, since they'd shared
beers with us. I'd made this breakfast a few times before
at campgrounds, and it was unhealthy but delicious. After
I got the fire going, I cooked the bacon in the pan, set
it aside to dry on paper towels, then drained about half
the grease. I'd stirred together the eggs and milk ahead

of time, and poured that into the pan, then sloshed the eggs back and forth with a spatula. When that was done I put the bagels I'd cut in half face-down in the rest of the grease, and yelled for everybody to get up.

"Smells good," Mike said, taking the plate I handed him. "Thanks."

We ate like a pack of dogs. A pound of bacon, a dozen eggs, and a couple of bagels was the perfect breakfast for four hungry climbers. We ate in silence, all of us wearing pile jackets against the morning chill. "Where's the coffee, Jordo?" A.J. asked.

"At Starbucks when we head through Leavenworth."

Took us another hour to clean up the campground, pack, and get going. We said goodbye to Mike and Brian and made vague plans to climb here again in September. We exchanged cell numbers so we could figure it out later.

We actually did stop at Starbucks for a couple of coffees, then headed east. We planned to go about five miles, turn south on Highway 97, then hook up with Interstate 90 east. Vantage is near the freeway—basically, it's the rocks above the Columbia River, right smack in the middle of the state.

I flipped on the blinker and was getting ready to turn when A.J., looking at the guidebook, said, "Hold up, Jordo. Keep going straight."

"Why?"

"Peshastin Pinnacles are just a couple more miles ahead. Let's take a quick climb before heading to Vantage."

I shrugged and said okay.

I'd heard of the Peshastin Pinnacles. They weren't climbed as much as the slabs in the Icicle were, at least not by the climbers at You So Mighty. They got killer hot after ten in the morning in the summer, I'd heard, and you didn't want to be anywhere near them. But since it was only a little after nine, I thought we should be okay for a short slab, even though the day was looking like a scorcher.

The Pinnacles were easy to spot on the north side of the highway, looming above an apple orchard. They looked really small compared to Snow Creek Wall. I parked and we grabbed our packs.

Also unlike Snow Creek, the Pinnacles were close to the road—a five-minute walk from the car. I mentioned what I'd heard about the heat to A.J., and he nodded.

"Yeah, the guidebook said the same thing," he said. "I've found a short one. Sunset Slab, just west of Dinosaur Tower. It's only a 5.6 friction route." He was pointing, and I saw where he meant.

I also saw that the rock was different here—tan sandstone rather than the gray granite I was used to. Not that it mattered. We could handle a 5.6 on marble under a waterfall.

It was one pitch to the ledge, two to the top. "Book says to just take the ledge to the left and descend on the anchors," A.J. said. "Good warm-up. Then we can decide if we want to do more or head out."

The way the sun was already hitting me, I thought we should just do the one-pitch and go. A.J. seemed to know the place, so he led. He went up the groove in the sandstone with ease. "We didn't need to rope up for this," he called down.

"You need to practice safe climbing and safe sex," I yelled up at him, and saw his teeth flash in a smile. "On belay?"

"Belay on."

"Climbing."

After Snow Creek, this route really was a breeze. I did notice the rock wasn't very good, and was glad we were roped—a chunk came off in my hand. A.J. did a good job of not dropping any of that crap on me.

I got to the ledge and took a seat next to him. "Not much to that," he said, hopping to his feet and starting north along the ledge. "Let me check the upper section over here." I nodded and got a bottle of water out of my pack. I took a sip and was looking at the other pinnacles, just chilling. I never looked over at A.J. and I'm not sure how much time passed—maybe two or three minutes. I was just getting to my feet when I heard him say, "N-aah!"

That's what it sounded like, anyway. Like he started to say, "No!" then added, "Ahh." I heard the combination, looked over and saw him falling sideways. Loose rocks came down with him. His right hip and leg hit the ledge as he passed, which slowed him slightly. He tried to grab hold, clawing for purchase, but was going too fast—and he kept going. Our eyes met for a split second and I saw fear and disbelief. I reached toward him but he was thirty feet away. He kept groping for the wall all the way down. He bounced three times off the slightly angled rock before he slammed into the ground at the bottom.

The sound was like a bag of dog food falling off a truck. I've had periodic nightmares about it ever since, and I always wake up in a sweat. A.J. was the best athlete I've ever seen, and it just seemed wrong that a shitty old theory like gravity could take him down.

I ran along the ledge. I still don't know how I down-climbed that rock as fast as I did without falling myself. A.J. was moving his hands a little and moaning when I got there. He was on his back, looking up at the rock that betrayed him, eyes half open and glazed. Blood was trickling from his mouth and his helmet was dented.

I just stood there for a moment, not sure what to do. Some other climbers had seen A.J. fall—or heard him land—and were running toward us.

"I called, an ambulance is on the way!" said a guy holding a cell phone.

"Shit, look at his leg!" said his partner. He turned aside and puked. A three-inch section of A.J.'s right leg bone was sticking out sideways above his knee.

I put my water bottle to A.J.'s mouth and he sipped a little. Then I thought of something. "It's bad," I said to the guy with the phone. "Can you call them back and see if he can get airlifted to Harborview?"

"Yeah, yeah, good idea."

He called the hospital back and talked while I gave A.J. some more water.

"The paramedics have to make that call. They said don't give him water or aspirin and don't move him. Just talk to him."

I talked to him but he didn't respond. His breathing was ragged and he spit blood a few times. His pulse was sluggish. The guy with the phone conveyed all this to the hospital. He stood over A.J. to keep him in his shadow— the day was getting hotter.

Paramedics from Leavenworth arrived in a few minutes, along with a state patrol officer. The paramedics immediately called for an airlift, and the patrolman said we should follow him down to the parking lot—he needed to get statements from us and we should get out of the way. Walking down the hill, I was dazed and half-stumbled a few times. Could I be dreaming? Was it possible I'd wake up in a few minutes, look over and see A.J. still snoozing in his sleeping bag?

"So what happened?" the patrolman asked when we got to his jeep.

The other guys looked at me, and then the officer did, too. "He led a pitch up Sunset Slab," I said. "No problem, and I came up after. I was resting for a minute and he said he wanted to check something out. I thought he meant just *look*. We were about to go down, you know? I stood up and then I saw him falling."

"Falling from the ledge?"

"No, that's what I mean—he climbed up a ways, without telling me. I saw him fall from at least fifteen feet before he hit the ledge, so he might've been twenty feet up when he lost it."

The patrolman nodded. "Some bad rock up there."

"Yeah, some came down with him. He hit the ledge for a second but kept going. I couldn't believe it, and he was too far away..."

He nodded and put his hand on my shoulder. "Have you notified your friend's family?"

"Uh, no."

"I'll call them now. Give me the number."

While the patrolman called, the other guys introduced themselves. Will and David, from Wenatchee. I thanked them for their help.

"No problem," David said. "Sorry about your friend..."

"Yeah, hope he'll be okay."

I heard A.J.'s mom yell for a second when the officer told her A.J.'s condition was "very serious." He told her to go to Harborview Medical Center in Seattle. He hung up and asked me more questions while he filled out an accident report. David and Will took off. Up the hill, the paramedics moved around A.J. About twenty minutes later I heard the helicopter.

It all happened fast. The helicopter hovered above the Pinnacles and lowered a secured stretcher. The paramedics loaded A.J. and up he went. The craft circled and was out of sight in a few seconds.

The paramedics brought A.J.'s pack down to the parking lot. "How was he?" I asked the woman.

"Not good," she said. "Fractured leg, internal injuries."

I waited for more, but she just looked at me for a moment with sad eyes and a pursed mouth, then turned and left. The patrolman asked me if I was okay to drive, and I told him yeah, I was, and got in the car and left. I wanted to be out of there.

In Leavenworth I pulled into a parking lot and called Mom, Pete, and Juana. Mom gasped and told me to drive straight home, like she thought I'd take a side trip to Oregon or something. Pete told me he'd meet me at the Streamside Bar and Grill in Sultan. I knew where he was talking about, since we'd stopped there a few times after climbs.

"Might have some news by then, Jordan," he said. "You'll lose reception in the mountains, and you need to focus on driving right now. You're upset, I can tell by your voice you're in shock, so just take it easy."

"Okay, Pete. See you in Sultan."

. . .

Juana didn't answer her phone, probably because she was still pissed. I left a brief message and said I'd call her when I got back to Everett.

Highway 2 was crowded. I just replayed the whole thing over and over again, wondering how it went wrong, what I could've done differently. I imagined making the turn onto 97 like we'd planned, and telling A.J. not to mess around on the rocks without being belayed.

When I snapped back to reality, I just worried. I'm not religious, but I prayed for him and swore to whatever gods might be listening that I'd be a much better person if he got through this. I didn't know what else to do.

Took me two hours to get to Sultan, and it felt like five. I saw Pete's car in the parking lot of Streamside. He was sitting on the deck, a beer bottle on the table in front of him. He walked over to me, a serious expression on his face.

"No good way to say it, Jordo," he said, putting his hand on my shoulder. "A.J. died on the way to the hospital."

. . .

I didn't cry. I'm not sure why—it just didn't happen. Maybe in the back of my mind I knew A.J. wasn't going to make it, so I was prepared for the news. He was half dead when I was sitting next to him. I looked back at the mountains to the east. All my life I'd been looking at them, aching to challenge them. They didn't care if they killed A.J. or anyone else, and for the first time I wasn't sure why I cared about climbing them so much.

Pete knew the waitress and she brought me a beer, too. "The hell with legal," she said. "I'm very sorry about your friend."

I felt numb. We drank our beers in silence, then ordered another pair. Before they arrived, Pete sighed and took off his red beret, revealing his bald top for the first time, at least to me.

"Freaks out my girlfriends when I do this," he said, placing the beret on the table. "One of them said it was like Darth Vader losing his mask."

He bent his head forward. A jagged scar, whiter than the skin around it, bisected his crown.

"Damn, Pete!"

"Yes, you can see why I keep my head covered. Fortunately, I like berets."

"So how did that happen?"

"My climbing partner at the time was a guy named Jack MacLaren. Do I have to add that he was Irish? Damn Mick bastard, a Frenchman should've known better than to partner with one of those wild-eyed whiskey swillers ... Actually, he was the best partner I ever had, and it was just an accident."

"Where were you?"

"Alaska, a pipsqueak of a peak in the Chugach Range called Flattop, right outside Anchorage. We were going for Denali and got up there a week early, and one day we decided to go up Flattop for a training hike. It's only a couple thousand feet, but the trail is steep, and there's some good scrambling on the north side. We left the trail on the west side and headed over."

He was shaking his head and looking down. "We heard later that the locals call the rock 'Chugach crud.' Really rotten shit, with all the weather they get up there. Anyway, Jack was leading, and he came to an easier segment and moved fast while I was stalled on a tricky section. Understandable mistake. He put his foot on a rock and it came loose when he was maybe thirty feet above me."

"Too far!"

"Damn right it was. That rock had some serious momentum. Jack yelled, 'Rock, rock! Shit, rock!' I remember hearing it exactly that way, very fast, and I had just enough time to look up and catch a glimpse. Damn thing was about the size of a loaf of bread and would've brained me if it hit directly at that speed. By luck it hit the edge of a protrusion about a foot over my head and spun past me at an angle—most of it. An edge caught me a glancing shot."

He looked me in the eye. "I could've died very easily. I fell ten feet and landed on a ledge with a patch of grass. What are the odds I'd have a soft landing? The combo of the fall and the rock knocked me out, and I bled like hell. Jack fixed me up as best he could and I came to in a few minutes. I was really out of it, a bad concussion, and he had a helluva time getting me down. My feet weren't cooperating."

He paused to sip his beer. I was already feeling light-headed from the first one so didn't drink much of the second. I hadn't eaten since that big breakfast—in another life.

"Some hikers saw us struggling," Pete continued, "and they came over to help, and one of them ran down to his car, drove a couple of miles to the first house he came to, and had them call an ambulance—this was pre-cell phone. The ambulance was in the parking lot by the time I arrived, and I was stuck in the hospital for three days. I was in no shape for Denali when I got out. Jack wanted to skip it and fly back with me, but I told him fuck no, he should climb. He hooked up with some other guys and summited."

"You were lucky."

"Yes, I was. The rock came within an inch or two of ending my life. An inch or two. And we were experienced and skillful climbers." He shook his head slightly.

"I think about that rock every day. And you know what, Jordo? I'm grateful to the cruddy piece of shit. Grateful as hell. I think of it as a blessing, even if I'm an ex-Catholic atheist. That rock made me consider my mortality and how I wanted to live the rest of my days. And I decided to live them to the lees."

He put his beer down and stood. "Mourn A.J., Jordan. Then start living again. Come on, let's head to town."

SEVENTEEN

Memory is an abstract painting—
it does not present things as they are,
but rather as they feel.

—Eugenia Collier

Mom hugged me when I came in the door. It was very obvious she'd been crying. She made me a sandwich, snuffling sometimes as she sliced the cheese and tomato, and sat on the couch while I ate at the table. It felt like I was starving, but then I couldn't eat more than a few bites.

After a long hot shower, I told Mom the story. She embraced me again when I was done. "Reporters have been calling," she said. "I told them our hearts go out to the Stevens family. That seemed appropriate. They didn't press for more because I didn't know anything else, but there's a good chance they'll call back tonight or tomorrow. We have to decide how to handle that."

"I don't feel like talking about it anymore," I said. "To anyone."

"That's fine with me," she said. "I'll just tell them 'No comment' if they call."

At six she used the remote to turn on the television. A.J. was a big story, since he was a football and track star. They had a picture of A.J.'s family huddled at the hospital, comments from a spokeswoman at Harborview, Coach Sadowski at Mountain View, and Casey and a couple other football players and students who had set up a vigil at the football field.

The phone started ringing after the segment, and didn't stop for hours. Mom screened the calls, answered a few, talked to friends, said "No comment" to reporters, and finally unplugged the phone at ten.

I called Juana on my cell. She was crying and we didn't have much to say, except how sorry we both were about our fight and A.J. We made plans to see each other the next afternoon. In bed, I kept replaying the day in my mind, especially the fall, and somehow fell asleep around midnight.

. . .

The story was in the papers Monday morning. They used the phrase "tragic accident" and included more details than the TV stories. The patrolman was interviewed along with local climbers familiar with the Peshastin Pinnacles. The Seattle papers said A.J. was climbing with a friend; the *Everett Journal-News* used my name. The phone kept ringing.

A couple of Internet hacks crucified me. It was bullshit lies—Jordan Woods fucked up a belay, pulled a rock down on A.J. Stevens, cut the rope. They had me doing everything but shooting him.

.   ▪   .

The memorial service was held Friday at the First Presbyterian Church in Everett. The story had gotten less coverage as the week progressed, but there were still TV cameras and reporters milling around the parking lot. Mom and I ducked inside before they could spot us.

Although we were ten minutes early, the church was already packed. Seating was mostly reserved. A.J.'s family was up front, of course, on the left side of the center aisle. Behind them was the whole football team. In front, on the right side of the aisle, were school administrators, board members, state and local politicians. Behind them were teachers, and behind them was a general student section.

I was in the lobby area, with maybe a hundred more students and other folks with some connection to A.J.

Juana was there, and she came over and hugged me and Mom. She held my hand and I felt a little better. We spotted Zenny and Pete on the far side of the lobby, along with a few other climbers from the gym and crags.

Juana noticed some of the unfriendly stares aimed my way. "Talk about *persona non grata*," she whispered.

"That's me," I agreed. A few minutes later a football player spotted me through the glass partition. Word spread and heads turned, and I saw mean, empty eyes before they turned away.

There were some great pictures of A.J. in the altar area, blown up big so everyone could see them. A.J. running the football...at a dance...acting in a school play...with his arm around his little sister...standing in front of his parents. A minister walked to the podium and began the service with a blessing and a summary of A.J.'s life. "Most of us don't accomplish in a full life what A.J. Stevens did in seventeen years," he concluded. "Look around at all the people he touched. We are all the richer for having known him, however briefly, and we are all the poorer because he was taken from us too soon."

A couple of the football players turned to glare at me again. Coach Sadowski spoke next, talking about A.J.'s personality being as important to the team as his talent, how he helped out the younger players, encouraged guys who were struggling. Then Casey spoke, telling a story about A.J. eating a burger and laughing so hard that a pickle slice shot out his nose. He laughed with everyone else, but it turned into a sob. He tried to talk more but his voice caught, and Sadowski and his dad walked him back to his seat.

After a couple more speakers, there was a slide show with music. More photos of A.J. in action—football, track, relaxing at school, lugging boxes in the food drive, hanging out with friends and family. No pictures of him climbing. I sort of understood, but still, climbing was a big part of his life and something he loved. If he'd died on the football field, would they have left out all those pictures?

The slide show left many people in tears, including Mom and Juana. The minister gave another blessing, and that was it. People began milling around. Juana wanted to beat the crowd and said she'd call me later. Zenny was making his way in our direction, and I was about to greet him when Mom took a step toward him and they embraced without a word. She hugged him hard and cried on his shoulder.

"You okay, Angie?" he asked. She sniffled and nodded. He turned toward me. "How you holding up, Jordan?"

"Uh, okay." I was shocked, and just told Mom I had to use the bathroom and I'd meet her outside.

When I was washing my hands, thinking about Mom and Zenny and wondering how they knew each other, the door of the bathroom opened. Ron Mears stepped inside. He put his index finger to his throat and made a slashing gesture. Then he walked out.

The lobby was packed and it took me awhile to get to

the doors—I wanted to be out of there. Just as I stepped outside, my eyes locked with Casey's. He looked at me like I was an opponent across the line from him, eyes as hard as granite.

.   .   .

Mom and I didn't talk on the way home—we were both absorbed in thought. We managed some soup for dinner. Neither of us had been eating much all week. After we cleaned up, Mom took a deep breath and said, "Jordan, we need to have a talk."

"Yeah," I said, "we do."

She went into her bedroom and came back with a photo album. She sat on the big couch with her legs folded under her.

"I haven't told you much about your father's death," she said, eyes welling. "You know it upsets me."

"Yeah. You don't have to ..."

"No, I do. I was wrong, Jordan. Here, look through this album. You haven't seen it before. I'm going to make myself a drink."

She handed me the album and went to the kitchen. It had pictures of Mom and Dad when they were young, in their early twenties. At a party, with my grandparents, on a boat. I flipped a page—and my mouth fell open. I looked up at Mom, returning to the couch with a glass of red wine.

"Why didn't you tell me?"

"Because I wanted to be a responsible parent," she said. "You're all I have left, kiddo."

The top picture showed Mom working her way up a cliff. Another showed her and Dad on top of a crag I recognized from Index Town Walls. There were many other photos, including one showing Dad and Zenny with their arms around each other's shoulders.

"Your father and I met climbing at Mount Erie," Mom said. "We knew right away it was meant to be, and we went back there every year on our anniversary."

I nodded, waiting.

"You've heard the story about you leaving the trailer while we were sleeping and climbing the cliff at Erie. Tom Mosher helped you down. You know him as Zenny. We stayed in touch and became friends with him, and after your father died … " She shrugged.

"All right, that explains part of it," I said. "How did Dad die?"

"He died on Pico D'Orizaba, the big volcano in Mexico," she said. "He was starting a guide service and that was his first trip out of the country. It was just bad luck. They were on their way down from the summit, there was an earthquake, and he and his two clients were killed by a rock fall. Just bad luck."

She put her head in her hands, sobbed for a second, took another deep breath, then looked up at me with red eyes. "The mountains have not been good to us," she said. "I lost my husband, you lost your father—and now your friend. I know you love to climb, Jordan, it's in your blood. But I simply can't lose you, too."

"I'm careful," I said weakly, and her eyes flashed with anger.

"So? You think your father was reckless? You think A.J. was?"

The truth was, A.J. was a little reckless. I'm sure Dad was a careful climber.

"I want you to make me a promise," she said. "I want you to promise me that you won't climb outdoor crags anymore. You can still climb at the gym and hike in the mountains. That's what sane people do. But no more rock climbing outdoors... Please Jordan, promise me!" Her face was a round mask of anguish. She dropped her head in her hands and cried harder than I'd ever seen her.

And I promised.

.   .   .

Mom went to bed early, before seven—and before I could ask her about some things on my mind. I left a note, in case she woke up, saying I was going out for a couple hours.

I drove through downtown Everett and got on Highway 2. Halfway across the trestle I took the Ebey Island exit. There was a place to park under the highway, close to the slough.

Ebey Slough is a smaller branch of the Snohomish River. I remembered Zenny telling me that he lived aboard an old houseboat around here. I found a path near the water and followed it north.

After a quarter-mile I came to a mini-marina consisting of two small sailboats and two slightly bigger houseboats. They were tied with ropes to each other and to trees on the shore. An outhouse was the only building in the area.

The slough had a leisurely current so the boats didn't seem in danger of going anywhere, though I thought that might be different during flood season in the spring.

The first houseboat had a red kayak on the deck next to a wooden statue of the Buddha in his meditation pose, so I figured it had to be Zenny's. I was about to step aboard the plank leading to the deck when he opened the door and smiled at me. He was holding a sketch pad and pencil.

"Hey, Jordan."

"Hi, Zenny. You got time to talk?"

"Sure, welcome aboard."

Inside, he told me again that he was sorry about A.J. I nodded and looked around. There were three rooms—a kitchen on one side, a bedroom on the other. The middle room was an art studio. A big canvas on an easel faced the eastern windows, beside a table with paints and brushes. Leaning against the walls were dozens of paintings, in stacks of six or so. To the right of the hatchway was a camping chair with two seats. A large cushion faced an altar on the other side—Zenny's meditation area, I guessed.

I looked closer at the painting. Splotches of yellow and red with an aquamarine background. It seemed violent and peaceful, moving and still, all at once.

"What is it?" I asked.

"Beats me," he shrugged. "I just paint 'em. I used to be more of a realist—and still am when the mood strikes. I sketch when I go kayaking around here, and I'm always finding good material. Mostly, though, I favor abstract art."

I remembered some wild abstract painting on the wall of the art room when I took Intro to Drawing as a freshman. "Does it bother you that people don't know what you're painting?"

"Not at all. They can interpret as they wish. Realism is okay, but I think the paint knows where to go better than I do."

I had to think about that one.

"I made the mistake," he continued, "of telling some of my climbing buddies that I'm an Abstract Impressionist. They decided to hear that as 'All-Star Exhibitionist,' and that's been their second-favorite nickname for me, after Zenny."

"I can relate," I said. "My nickname is Monkey Boy."

"Climbers, huh? Hey, you want a glass of water? That's the only beverage available aboard the vessel Ship Faced."

"What?"

He smiled. "Yeah, Ship Faced, take a look near the bow"—he pointed north—"before you leave. Not the name I gave her. I found her abandoned and in bad shape about a mile north of here. Salvaged ol' Ship Faced and moved her over here. Thought about changing the name, but I heard that's bad luck."

"It's a cool place to live," I said.

"I like it and it suits me." He shrugged. "But most people consider it a step above homeless."

"You're an artist, so you're supposed to live out of the mainstream, right?"

"Well, many artists don't fit in very well. Two of my neighbors are also artists—a musician and a writer. A retired couple lives on one of the sailboats. We all value a simple, quiet existence, and we've been a community for over a decade."

I'd been waiting for an opening. "Is that why you never married my mom?" I asked. "Incompatible life-styles?"

He looked at me with his deep-set eyes. I expected denial or anger, something. He was still calm old Zenny.

"She told you?"

"Sort of. I saw a picture of you and my dad in an album. And then there was the way you two hugged at A.J.'s service today. I kind of knew she had a boyfriend that she didn't talk about."

He nodded. "First, Jordan, let me say that I love your mother very much. And she loves me, too."

"So why didn't you get married, or at least live together?"

"Well, despite our mutual affection, we're both stubbornly independent. I like the way I live, Angie likes the way she lives, and yes, we are not compatible in that sense. She doesn't approve of my lifestyle and wants me to move to town and get a real job. You should've seen the expression on her face when I first showed her the community restroom."

I nodded, smiling a little. "Mom can be a little snooty sometimes."

He shrugged. "In any case, we can't seem to work out an arrangement to put us under the same roof. It's caused most of our arguments. We've broken up dozens of times over the years, and I know she'd like to find a more compatible guy. Then again, she's dated guys who are more her type, but she ends up dumping them. And we get back together after a month or two apart."

"I still don't get why she kept this a secret from me."

"Well, in addition to our contrasting lifestyles, I'm a climber. She didn't want you to have a father figure who would encourage you to hit the crags, which I naturally would have. That's been another source of tension between us."

I thought it over. It was all beginning to make sense.

"She wants me to quit climbing," I said. "Except maybe in the gym. And only go hiking in the mountains."

"Understandable reaction, after what happened."

"Yeah, I guess."

"Give her some time, Jordan. Maybe you should stay off the crags for now. Next summer you'll be out of school, eighteen years old, and you can do what you want. Why don't you go along with Angie for now, then bring it up again next spring, after you've both had time to heal?"

Had to admit that made sense. "I was a little mad at you," I said. "But I get it now. And I wanted to thank you for saving me when I was a little kid."

"Hey, no big thing, Jordan. I just had the gear and they didn't, or they would've gone up after you. That's how we became friends. I was glad to help."

"I figure that Mom probably had you keep an eye on me out in Index, too."

"Yeah, I plead guilty."

I nodded. "Well," I said, "I should get going."

When I was back on the riverbank, he said, "There's a quote attributed to Jesus in the Gospel of Thomas that I like. Want to hear it?"

"Sure."

"Jesus said, 'If you bring forth what is within you, what you bring forth will save you. If you do not bring forth what is within you, what you do not bring forth will destroy you.'"

I looked at a branch floating slowly by and thought about that.

"You honor your parents best by using your gifts," Zenny added. "Even if your gifts do involve some risk. Accidents happen crossing the street, too. Statistically, climbing is safer than driving a car, especially if you climb smart. Look at Ed Viesturs—he scaled the biggest mountains in the world and always came back safe and sound. You could be that kind of climber, too."

"Thanks, Zenny... I mean, Tom."

He smiled. "Zenny is fine," he said. "And it's a helluva lot better than All-Star Exhibitionist."

EIGHTEEN

Freedom's just another word for
nothing left to lose.

—Kris Kristofferson

A week before school started, I told Mom I wanted to transfer to Kamiak High in Mukilteo. "I'm sure I could get a variance."

"Jordan, you've gone to school for three years at Mountain View, and I think you should graduate from there, with all your friends."

"I don't have any friends there anymore," I said. "Except Juana. Everybody else is either a friendly acquaintance or an enemy. And right now I have a lot more enemies."

"You can't run away from your problems," she said. "You have to stand up to them. You've stood up to bullies your whole life, and now is not the time to stop."

I rolled my eyes. "Mom, you don't get it!"

She poured herself a cup of coffee and sat at the table, being so calm it was annoying. "You're overreacting," she said. "And I think you're feeling a little sorry for yourself. This will blow over."

"Mom . . ."

"Just start school, and we'll talk about it again in a week."

. . .

I was worried about Juana catching some of the crap aimed at me, so I wrote her a letter and formally broke up with her before Labor Day weekend. You can't text someone a breakup message, and talking on the phone would've been too hard.

We were sort of drifting apart anyway. She hadn't come by the gym, and I'd only seen her a few times since the funeral. We went out twice for sad talks at Starbucks, and I met her for dinner once, down at the restaurant where she worked. That was it.

She told me she'd been angry after our argument and had accepted a date with a guy she worked with, the next night, when A.J. and I were camping at the Icicle. They'd seen each other a few times since, she said, but it wasn't a big deal.

I was so numb that it didn't break my heart the way it would've under different circumstances. The heart can only handle so much sadness at a time. That's one thing I learned.

Well, anyway, I wrote her a nice letter, telling her how much I cared about her and admired her, but that we should go our separate ways. I stood at the mailbox at the Everett Post Office for a few minutes after dropping the letter inside, wondering if I did the right thing.

The first day of school was the Tuesday after Labor Day. I snuck around campus, avoiding the clumps of football players I spotted. Matt Bird said hi, he was sorry to hear about A.J., and I thanked him. Most students looked at me strangely, though, and some moved across the hall to avoid walking too close. A few football players spotted me after second period and did the throat-slash gesture. They were smiling slightly, but the smiles weren't friendly and their eyes were cold and mean.

It was like a mighty wall had sprung up between me and the rest of the world. I stayed close to the real school walls and moved fast between classes, wary of an ambush. I saw a few football dudes clearly planning one after third period, and took off running.

My fourth period class was Calculus with Mrs. Klein, and I entered her room with a sliding cut after an all-out sprint, looking back at the posse of football players chasing after me. I was the first to arrive and took a seat in back. Billy Briggs tried to follow me in, but Mrs. Klein, standing by her door, put her hand on his chest and told him to go to his own class.

He got disrespectful with her, and I saw her wagging her finger in his face and heard the words "referral" and "suspension" a few times. He pointed a finger at me and gave Mrs. Klein an ugly stare as he left. After taking attendance, she walked back to her desk and wrote up a referral, looking pissed off.

I wasn't focused in a math class—for the first time, well, ever. Near the end, Mrs. Klein asked me to step out in the hall for a moment and to bring my stuff. Everyone did a sarcastic "ooo-ahhh" thing. Sarcastic because it was the first day and I hadn't said a word, so they knew I couldn't be in trouble, at least not the usual kind of trouble.

I was sort of shocked when she hugged me, out in the hall. "Jordan," she said, her hands on my shoulders and looking me in the eyes, "I'm so sorry about A.J., and I think it's terrible and cowardly that some are blaming you."

"Yeah, that's the problem."

"Have you told your parents?"

"My mom. She thinks I'm exaggerating, that I should tough it out."

"I'll call her, and also let Principal Denny know what's going on."

"Uh, I'm not sure that will help. Might even make it worse … I don't know."

"Trust me, Jordan, you want all the help you can get right now. I'll talk to the principal when I turn in that referral for Billy Briggs. And you need to talk to your mom after I do. Tell her about what happened today. I'm sure she'll listen if we double-team her."

She looked at her watch and told me I could leave early for lunch. I ran across campus and was at the metro bus stop before the bell rang.

■   ■   ■

At home, I had a Coke and thought it over. I was pissed at Mom but didn't want her to worry too much, so I wrote her a note. Writing seemed to be the only way I could communicate anymore.

Dear Mom,

Sorry, but I gotta go. If I stay around here this week there's a good chance I'm going to be dead or in the hospital. The word on the street is that I killed A.J. or at least that I'm the one responsible for his death, and since he was like a god, not to mention the most popular person in town, I'm fucked. Sorry about the language, Mom, but it's true. Some of his football buddies are after me, and his track and drama friends want to beat me up, too.

Well, maybe the actors would only glare and yell and emote at me. I left it in anyway.

I'll call you in a week or so, after things settle down, and let you know how I am. Please don't worry. I just need to think and get away from all the hate.
Love,
Jordan

I knew she'd worry even though I told her not to. That's the way moms are.

I didn't want Pete to rat me out before I was out there, so I decided to wait to text him. I wouldn't be able to get through once I was in the mountains, so I'd do it from the bus, and I wouldn't tell him where I was heading. Although I trusted Pete with just about everything, this was a different situation. I knew he'd feel obligated to tell Mom where I was.

Just like with Rainier, I loaded my big pack with some of the same stuff—sleeping bag, pad, compass, map, sunglasses, gloves, wool cap. I left out the crampons and ice axe, and added my tent, two bottles of water, water filter, and toilet paper. Then I rolled three sets of clothes and rain gear real tight—rolling clothes saves space in a pack—and grabbed a bunch of packets of raisins, a few granola bars, an unopened can of nuts, and box of crackers. I'd get more later. I debated grabbing my hiking boots, but decided it would be too much weight—I'd just stick with my running shoes.

The pack was brimmed out and heavy, probably forty pounds or more. I usually forget something on trips, but I checked it over and it seemed pretty well covered. So I buckled it up and headed out the door, feeling half guilty and half excited.

I walked over to the bus depot in about ten minutes. I got a hundred bucks out of the ATM there, for food and travel back. Couldn't think of anything else I would need, so that was more money than necessary, but it seemed like a good idea. The bus ticket was only a few dollars—gotta like Sound Transit. My timing was good; I only had to wait about ten minutes.

I watched the cows on Ebey Island east of town. No fences out there, and I remembered driving to Index with A.J. and him joking that they were wild cows. He'd started making up a song about them, to the tune of the Rolling Stones' "Wild Horses." I couldn't remember the lyrics, but we'd both contributed a few lines to pass the time, and had a pretty funny song by the time we reached Index Town Walls.

I sent Pete a text, real basic. I felt bad not trusting him with the whole story.

Because of all the stops, it took over an hour to get to Gold Bar, about thirty miles east of Everett. I could see my destination from the bus—a vertical white slash on a dark green mountainside. A tourist might mistake it for snow at first glance, but I knew it was Wallace Falls.

I bought some peanut butter, cheese in a can, cookies, and more crackers at a store, and along with the stuff I brought from home, I had enough for a week. No hot food—I didn't want the weight of a stove, and smoke from a campfire might attract attention. After a week of this stuff, I'd be dying for a burger.

I had to walk about a mile or so through town to get to the trailhead in the state park. I was glad it was a weekday afternoon because the trail gets crowded on weekends, especially in the early fall. The last thing I needed was to get spotted by any folks I knew, and I was always running into them on this trail. They'd get suspicious that I was on my own, and more suspicious if I ignored them.

The trail passes under humming electrical towers, then into the woods. There's a sign, nailed to a hemlock tree, that I sort of like: *Come forth into the light of things*, it says. *Let nature be your teacher*. It's by a poet named Wordsworth—Juana could probably tell me all about him, if I ever talked to her again. Anyway, it looked like nature was going to be my only teacher at the beginning of this school year.

It's a little under two miles to the lower falls, mostly uphill and sometimes steep, but I covered it in less than a half hour. Usually I'm pretty friendly on the trail, but this time I kept my cap low and my head down and ignored the half-dozen hikers who passed me on their way back to the parking lot, as well as the three hikers I overtook. I glanced at them but didn't recognize anyone. So far, so good.

I didn't stop to take pictures of the lower falls, or the middle falls—which is the real postcard, over one hundred feet high, the slash visible from the highway. Mom would've been going on about the glorious power and roaring beauty for five minutes. I just kept walking.

The trail gets steep after the middle falls, discouraging most hikers, and I started to feel that I'd made a clean getaway and could relax a little. About a quarter mile past the upper falls, three miles from the trailhead, is a dirt logging road. Turn left and it takes you to Wallace Lake. Right just goes a few hundred feet, to the river. I crossed the road into the woods and bushwhacked about a hundred yards until I found a little clearing. The dense trees prevented anyone from seeing me from the road, and the river was a stone's throw away, ripping along but not roaring like at the falls. Perfect.

I set up my tent. The fast hike had left me sweaty and I took off my shirt to dry. Most of the bugs were gone for the year, fortunately. I drank some water and stretched out to relax on top of my sleeping bag and pad, using my backpack as a pillow. And fell asleep.

I woke up about an hour later and started reading *Between a Rock and a Hard Place*—the book about Aron Ralston, who got his arm pinned by a boulder when trekking alone in Utah. He ended up cutting through his wrist to free himself and walked out, weak and a bloody mess. Made my problems seem pretty minor, though I could relate to the title.

After an hour of reading, I drank some water and ate peanut butter on crackers for dinner. It was so quiet—just a chirping goldfinch and the river. Still, I wished I'd grabbed my iPod for a little entertainment. I always forget something.

I went out to pee and look around a little. A good spot, no doubt. I walked over to the river. I could see where the upper falls started about a quarter mile downstream. I could hear them a little from the riverbank, though not from my tent. I went back to the tent and read until I fell asleep.

The next morning was cold, and I stayed cuddled in the sleeping bag for a half hour before my bladder forced me to get up and get dressed. I put on my rain gear for a little extra warmth and left the tent. The sun hadn't cleared the tops of the mountains yet, and wouldn't for at least a couple of hours. It'd be cool till then.

Back at the tent, I ate cheese and crackers for breakfast and read for a couple of hours. Every now and then I'd put down the book and think. Really didn't do me much good. I was torn between going back home and heading south for the winter, maybe to Arizona or New Mexico. I could get a job in an outdoor shop, climb at the local crags, and maybe get my GED. Stay away from the assholes who wanted to kill me. I mean, Mom had no idea—some of those guys would stomp on your head when you were on the ground, kick your teeth in, and go away laughing about it. No, part of me wanted to get away and start fresh. I'd be eighteen in February, so I was old enough to head out on my own.

Then I'd think about Juana and Mom and Pete and I'd feel lonely and guilty, though I think they'd understand. Well, maybe not Mom, with her "go to school and stand up for yourself" bullshit. She didn't get it. I mean, how do you stand up to a football team when you're five-seven and a buck-forty?

Maybe my note and Mrs. Klein's phone call would clear it up for her.

I was pretty restless by ten o'clock, so I got up and filled my fanny pack—the top of my big pack, which detaches—with my last water bottle, cheese, and a granola bar. I looked at the map. The dirt road I'd passed headed northwest to Wallace Lake, maybe two miles away. A four-mile hike would kill a few hours, anyway, and I'd never been to the lake, just the falls.

It was easy walking along the road and I was at the lake pretty fast. I sat at a picnic table and ate my lunch, looking out over the cattails at the still water. Some clouds had moved in, and the water reflected the grayish blue above. Nobody was up here on an overcast Wednesday.

I walked back, thinking about Zenny. He told me once that Zen was really just being aware in every moment. But that was tougher than it sounded. I could be totally aware when I was climbing, because you were always, in the back of your head, concerned about falling. A.J. said that a lot of sports were like that. "You daydream on the football field," he'd said, "and a linebacker brings you back to reality real quick."

Hiking along through the woods, though, my mind drifted all over the place, just like it did in English and History class and lots of other times. I sort of picked my Zen spots.

I mention that 'cause I was remembering making love to Juana when the black bear stepped out of the woods, about forty feet in front of me. I totally froze. I was about to take off, because the bear was looking right at me and kind of snorting. I knew that if it was a mama bear with cubs I'd be in deep shit—and I might be bear shit in a short while, if she was one of those rare bruins that attacks with intent to consume. I started backing away, and the bear suddenly ran across the road and into the woods on the other side. I waited a minute before I headed up the road again, my heart pounding hard.

I was smelling pretty bad after the hike. I'd showered the morning before, but that was almost forty hours and two hikes ago, so after dropping my pack in the tent, I went over to the river. I felt sort of nervous about getting naked even though I was deep in the woods—probably two miles from the nearest human, if a hiker was on the upper-falls trail. More likely I was five miles from anyone. Still, I took a good look around before I dropped my underwear and stepped into the cold water.

I had a splash bath, throwing water onto my face and hair and then the rest of my body, and scrubbing with my hands. Of course I forgot to bring a towel from home, so I dried off with a clean shirt. There was a chilly breeze and I was shivering when I got back to the tent. I zipped myself into the sleeping bag and read some more. There was enough book and food left to get me through tomorrow, I decided, then I'd hike out to the service station in Gold Bar Friday morning, get some more food and a paperback or two, and maybe call Mom ... maybe. I still hadn't figured out my next move. Just before I fell asleep, I realized that this was the first day in my life—at least as far back as I could remember—that I hadn't seen or talked to another human being.

On Thursday morning I felt like having a real workout. I checked the map and saw a couple of peaks to the northeast: Mount Stickney and Prospect Peak. They were on the same ridge, less than a mile apart, so I thought I'd knock them both off. I had my pack loaded and was on my way by seven.

While Mount Stickney was only about three miles away, there wasn't any trail to it, at least none that I found. So I bushwhacked through alder and salmonberry, which is no fun and real slow. Took me an hour to go the first mile. The elevation gain was steady, and finally I made it to rocks and could move at a better pace, even though it was a little steeper. The sky was overcast and the wind picking up a little, but it felt good on my face.

The first summit I saw for Stickney turned out to be false, and so did the second. The third one was the real deal. On top at last, I sat down and drank some water, put on another layer to keep the sweat chills away, and looked out over the Skykomish River Valley at the green-blue peaks to the south. I ate some cheese and crackers and a granola bar for lunch, thinking about how good hot food would taste when I treated myself tomorrow to lunch in Gold Bar.

After about forty minutes or so, I did a map check and decided to head north along the ridge to Prospect, which looked deceptively close and just a little higher than Stickney, though it was more like five hundred feet higher and close to a mile away.

About ten minutes later, everything got weird.

I'd noticed more clouds moving in while I rested on Stickney, but hadn't worried too much. I have a good sense of direction and know how to use a map and compass, so there was no way I could get lost—I thought.

Before I realized it the clouds had moved in low and fast, and I was in a whiteout. I've been in them a few other times in the mountains and wasn't too worried. The rule was, you don't climb what you can't see. This was an easy ridge walk, though, and I figured the sun would probably burn off the clouds by mid-afternoon at the latest. I kept heading north.

After a half hour, I was surprised to see that I wasn't going uphill toward the summit. I was still on a fairly level ridge. Just as I was about to check my map, the whiteout cleared a bit—and I was so shocked that I fell down.

I was looking at the Skykomish Valley, which I knew—knew!—was behind me, to the south. This was almost the exact same view I'd had at lunch—and it just couldn't be.

It felt like I'd stepped into a fantasy world, like Alice in Wonderland or something. Always before, the world was so logical and predictable. Then it went upside down out in Leavenworth in July, and now it was backwards. I sat there for ten minutes trying to figure out the mystery, feeling pretty freaked out. I thought I might be losing my mind, and started crying for the first time since A.J. died. I thought about him being gone forever and cried harder, my chest shaking and my throat all tight, and I felt more lonely and sad and confused than I ever had in my life. Part of me wanted to just walk into the whiteout until I fell off a cliff.

"I'm sorry, A.J.!" I sobbed into the void. "I'm so sorry!"

Finally I sort of pulled myself together. I drank some water and checked the map. I saw the contour I'd been following north toward Prospect, and the general area where I would've been when the clouds moved in—and then I spotted it. The ridge splits, very gradually. The left side continues north to Prospect, while the right side, which I'd obviously followed, curls northeast, then east, then southeast and finally south. Very strange to *know* you were facing north and find out it was actually south. This wrong ridge ended with tight contours—a cliff really was close.

More clouds moved in, and I could only see about forty feet or so. I just wanted to get back to my tent. Using the map and compass, I retraced my steps. It was slow going because I had to be careful. Sometimes the whiteout thickened and I could only see a few feet in front of me. Took me twice as long to get back to the lunch spot.

Usually you go down about twice as fast as you go up, but everything was off this day. It took me all afternoon to hack my way back through the dense foliage. I couldn't find the semi-path I'd made on the way up.

I was relieved when I finally saw parts of the river I recognized, and then my tent.

And just as I was shuffling off my pack, I heard a familiar voice.

NINETEEN

I hadn't cared if I got to the top. Just being
in the heart of the mountains was unearthly.
It was enough. It was complete. I was filled
with an acceptance of things just as they are,
which is grace.

—Richard Leo

Let's try through here," the deep voice said. "Looks like someone bushwhacked recently."

"Okay," came the answer—and I recognized my mother's voice. Before I could stop myself, I called out to them.

"Hey Mom, Pete!" I yelled. "Over here!"

I caught a glimpse of them moving through the trees.

Then they were at my campsite. Mom grabbed me in a hug. "Jordan, Jordan," she said. "You had us so worried!"

She finally let go and looked at me with her hands on my shoulders. "Are you okay? You're sweaty."

"Yeah, I'm fine, just getting back from a hike."

Pete stepped forward. "Think you can get out of work that easy?" he asked. And he gave me a quick hug as we laughed.

"How'd you find me?"

Mom said, "We figured you'd head out this way, either here or Index. You didn't take your car so the bus seemed logical. A driver remembered dropping a kid with a pack at Gold Bar."

"Pretty good detective work," I said. "I didn't even make it three days."

"Long enough to scare me half to death," she said with a critical tone.

"I might've been dead if I stayed home."

"Damn punks, " Pete said. "Just pure harassment."

He added that my tent didn't look big enough for the three of us, so we should start back. They told me to relax, and I sat on a stump and drank water while they packed up my gear. I wasn't really looking forward to more hiking, but still, there was a hot meal waiting at the end of this one. I almost started drooling just thinking about it.

They had my stuff ready to go in a few minutes. Pete cinched the tent to his pack, which made my load lighter, and we started through the woods.

Pete walked ahead when we reached the trail, and it was wide enough that Mom could walk next to me. "I'm sorry I didn't take the threats seriously," she said, looking a little sad, staring down at the trail. "I talked to the principal and your math teacher, and heard enough to understand why you took off. Wish you'd talked with me more."

"I tried, remember?" I said, feeling a little angry.

"Fair enough," she said. "I should've listened."

It was mostly downhill on the way back, and we made good time. We were all hungry by the time we reached the trailhead, and Pete suggested we stop at a Mexican restaurant in Sultan. "They're used to catering to smelly hikers and climbers, so we'll fit right in," he said. "Since I'm driving, too, you really don't have a choice."

At the restaurant, I ordered a large chicken burrito and put away a load of chips. Mom and Pete each had a Dos Equis. We were all pretty ripe and the waitress joked that they were going to install showers for folks coming off the trail. "We might also divide up the place into sweating and non-sweating sections."

I attacked my burrito when it came. Nothing had ever tasted so delicious. I ordered a second serving of rice and beans, too.

When he dropped us off, Pete said I was scheduled on Friday from three to six. "I'll be there," I said. "Thanks for coming after me."

"Gotta hang on to the good employees," he said. "See you at the gym."

At home, I took a hot shower. Mom got out of her shower a little later and came into the living room. "We have an appointment with the principal tomorrow, along with that boy and his parents," she said.

I nodded, too tired to argue.

• • •

The meeting was at nine in the morning. I had a talk beforehand with Principal Denny and filled in some gaps. Then Billy walked into the meeting room with his dad, and I saw he'd had to dress up a little, too. Mom was wearing a black business suit and looked pissed off.

"Thanks for coming, everyone," Principal Denny said when we were all seated. "I hope we can resolve this issue today."

"Billy served his suspension," Mr. Briggs said. "I don't see why he just can't return to classes today as usual."

"I want to make sure we don't have a recurrence of the harassment," the principal said.

"There will be no recurrence," Mr. Briggs said, looking at his son, who was avoiding his eyes. "Will there, Billy?"

He shrugged and mumbled something that might have been "No." Or maybe it was, "I don't know."

"The policy on bullying and intimidation is very clear," Denny said. "We have a teacher who witnessed an attempted assault. And according to Jordan, the players have chased him on at least two occasions and used a throat-slash gesture."

"Why don't you pick on somebody your own size?" Mom said to Billy.

"It's not my fault he's a little pipsqueak."

"It's not my fault you're a big asshole," I said. His mouth pinched shut and I could tell he had to keep himself from jumping across the table.

"Enough, both of you!" shouted Denny, red in the face. "Mr. Briggs, if Billy is involved in another bullying incident on campus, he'll be expelled and will not graduate from this school."

"And I already told you, Billy won't be a problem here."

"How about off campus?" Mom asked.

"That's a matter for the police," Denny said.

"The police aren't going to get involved in kids scrapping a little," Mr. Briggs said.

"It's not kids scrapping," Mom said. "It's called assault. And if that gorilla comes near my kid again, I have some friends who are going to put him in the hospital."

The room was deadly quiet for a second. Then Mr. Briggs was on his feet yelling and pointing a finger at Mom, and Billy and I stood up, and Principal Denny was trying to get everyone settled down. The yelling stopped when Officer Michaels stepped into the room.

"Thanks for coming," Denny said.

"Sorry I'm late," the cop said, looking at Mom and

Mr. Briggs. Both of them slowly sat down. "Looks like we have a situation here."

"We do indeed."

"Wait a minute," Mr. Briggs said. "You heard her. She just threatened my kid."

"Because your kid is threatening mine."

"For the third time, Billy is not going to do anything," his father said, looking at him hard. "Except go to school."

"I hope that's the case," Michaels said, "because I'm going to have Mrs. Woods and Jordan fill out a restraining order. I believe Principal Denny has explained that Billy will be expelled for the rest of the year if there's a problem on campus. And if he comes within a hundred feet of Jordan off school grounds, he'll be arrested."

Billy had his head down. "Look at me, son," Michaels said, and slowly Billy looked up. "Are we clear?"

"I guess."

Michaels kept staring. "Are we clear?" he repeated.

Something in the tone seemed to scare Billy. He nodded and said, "Yes, sir."

I didn't believe him. And I could read his mind. "What about his friends on the football team?" I asked.

Officer Michaels turned to me. "Try to steer clear of them," he said. "There's a lot of anger over A.J. Stevens, and right or wrong, people are blaming you. That's an unfortunate reality. Time passes, and things will get easier. Till then, don't isolate yourself here or off school grounds.

Go to school, go home. Lying low is the best advice I can give you, Jordan."

.   .   .

I saw Juana at lunch, sitting at a table with her tall friend Laura Burbach and a couple of other girls. I grabbed a sandwich and headed for the library area. The cafeteria is too small for everyone, even with all the students spread out over three lunches, so we're allowed to eat in the hallways around the library, which is in the same building. I sat on the floor just outside the door, a fairly safe and inconspicuous spot. I'd see anyone approaching me.

It surprised me when I looked up and saw Juana. "Mind if I join you?" she asked.

"Sure."

She gave me a little smile and plopped down. "I heard about you taking off for Gold Bar. You okay?"

"I've been better."

"Senior year's not shaping up like you expected, huh?"

"Nope," I said. "It sucks."

She nodded. "I got your letter. I was a little hurt, even though you said nice things about me."

"Probably shouldn't have sent you that," I said. "Sort of redundant, since we weren't really going out anymore."

"I thought we were just taking a break while you healed. And you know I was mad at you before that, for blowing me off when you went to the Icicle."

"Yeah, sorry. I was pretty mad, even though you were just being honest with me."

"I was," she said. "And you disappointed me by not seeing my side of things. I thought you were the perfect guy and we were meant for each other and all that. So I was planning out our future together, and didn't see how it could work if you were doing three to five years for burglary."

I actually laughed a little, surprised that I still could. "Sorry I disappointed you, Juana."

She put her hand on my arm. "No, it's okay. I figured out some things. I was disappointed in you because of my expectations. And no one can ever live up to someone else's expectations. I needed to let you be you, and not try to stop you from climbing Miami Beach high rises if that's your thing. I mean, I wouldn't want you telling me how to live, so why should I tell you?"

I thought about that. "I see what you mean," I said. "My expectations were that you'd come back to the gym and not want to see other guys, so I was disappointed in you, too."

"Do you think everything would be fine with us if we both dropped our expectations?"

"I don't know." I shrugged. "We could try and see how it works. I've never thought about it. I haven't done the relationship thing before, so I'm still learning."

"Me, too," she said. "But I know you're my best friend and I want to try to work things out with us. I want me and you to be a 'we' again."

The bell rang. We stood and smiled at each other, then kissed. We were heading in separate directions for fifth period, but it felt like we were heading the same way otherwise.

TWENTY

*I imagine that one of the reasons people cling
to their hates so stubbornly is because they
sense, once hate is gone, that they will be
forced to deal with pain.*

—James Baldwin

A s soon as I heard the sound, I knew I was in trouble.
I heard it when I was walking out of You So Mighty
just after six, heading down the block toward my car. I
was thinking about some things Pete had said. He'd asked
me how I was doing as I was leaving.

"Okay." I'd shrugged.

"Looks like you're still mourning, Jordo. It's been
almost two months."

"Am I just supposed to stop thinking about him?" I asked, a little angry.

Pete nodded. "Yes, for now that would be best. Revisit A.J. later. You don't want to make a habit of sad thoughts. They just go round and round and don't do you any good."

"I can't help it."

"Is that true? If you don't control your thoughts, who does?"

I shrugged and looked away.

"I told you about that rock that almost quelled me," he continued. "But did I tell you about my deathbed fantasy?"

"Uh, no."

"Well, ideally, I'd like a Catholic priest to give me the last rites. Preferably a guilty Irish priest. And as he bends over me in prayer, I spring up with my remaining strength, snare the whackjob bastard by the larynx with my five good teeth, and rip him to bloody shreds."

"Geez, Pete!"

"Yes, a rather violent fantasy, I admit. I'm very hard on priests. But I think it would be a fine way to exit this world ... Anyway, that's a tangential anecdote. My point, Jordo, is that the rock made me consider my mortality. I'd thought about heaven and nirvana and all that, and concluded that they might exist but I wasn't willing to take Pascal's Wager or trust in Buddhist Rebirth or any other bullshit theory. What's your take on life after death?"

His eyes were boring into me, and I looked away and shrugged. "I don't know."

"Honest answer. I'll tell you, though, what I know for sure is that I'm alive, right now. I don't want to throw it away climbing some damn wall to prove something to myself or anyone else. Not counting A.J., I've lost three good friends who were involved in that testicular madness. On the other hand, at least they were out there living when they fell. That's a better way to go than in front of a TV or lying in a hospital bed, waiting for the last beep on a monitor."

I nodded in agreement. Dying while climbing made a certain amount of sense to me, although I didn't want to go out doing something truly dumbass.

"I also don't want to waste time doing crap that other people think I should be doing," Pete continued. "Like trying to impress the neighbors with the size of my house. What watery excrement! No, I want to watch the sun rise over the Cascades, listen to the rain and the laughter of climbers in this place, drink delicious wine with some fine cheese, and, most of all, make love to big-breasted women!"

That was the second time I'd laughed since the Pinnacles, so maybe I was coming back to life.

"Most climbers are leg men," Pete continued. "Pure pragmatists. Not me. I'll take a fine rack every time."

"Does Marie know this?"

"Of course, and she has a fine rack, you may have noticed."

"But you used the word 'women.' Plural."

"Ah yes, monogamy. Marie initially threw a coffee mug at me when I voiced my views on that topic. But really, I think the whole one-true-love scenario is romantic horse-shit. A man can love many women. I've always thought the union should be about compatibility rather than love. Many couples ostensibly in love find, quite often, that they aren't compatible at all."

I'd thought about Mom and Zenny when he said that.

"Now Marie," he continued, "wants exclusivity, as most women do. We are quite compatible. And although I do enjoy the sight of a spry young gal working a wall, I've decided to marry her and be a faithful husband." After I congratulated him, he winked at me. "Of course, faithful to a Frenchman means one wife and one mistress."

. . .

Anyway, walking down the sidewalk, I didn't notice the van pull up behind me. I did hear the door open—that harsh sliding sound—and that's when I intuitively knew I was in trouble.

By the time I started running, it was too late. I got maybe three steps before I was tackled. Tackled hard. My right shoulder hit the sidewalk first, and I bounced and scraped along for a couple of feet. Then hands were grabbing me, excited voices surrounded me, and I was picked up and shoved in the van.

A second later someone gagged my mouth with a rolled-up T-shirt and covered my eyes with a blindfold, probably another shirt. I felt a moment of panic, then found I could breathe through my nose okay. I took deep inhalations and tried to remain calm.

Calm was tough, because the players were psyched that their plan had half-succeeded. They were cheering and slapping palms—and me. I couldn't brace for the blows because I couldn't see them coming. Suddenly I'd get slapped hard on the arm, the back of the head, across the face. I was struggling to keep it together and not cry.

They didn't drive very far. I felt the van turning, maybe four or five times. It was a short distance, and I was probably in the van less than ten minutes, but it seemed like a cross-country trip.

When the van stopped, the rough hands grabbed me again and carried me into a place that smelled of sawdust and motor oil. A garage? They tossed me into a chair, and grabbed my hands and tied them behind my back. Then they removed the blindfold and gag.

Yup, a garage, with a workbench to my right and a small window in front of me that let a little light into the dim space. Six football players stood around and glared at me.

"Aren't you going to yell and scream like a little girl?" Billy Briggs asked. I knew that asshole would be here. "Go ahead, won't do you any good. We tested it. The sound doesn't travel more than a few feet, and nobody's home."

"You guys sure you want to get arrested?" I asked.

They laughed, but there was a little fear in there, too. That could help me. "You let me go now," I continued, "and I promise I won't say a word. You don't, and you're all going to be charged with assault and kidnapping."

Less laughter, less sure. "No, that ain't how it's going down," said Briggs, stepping close and leaning down to put his face in mine. "If you say one word after you get out of the hospital, the second team moves in."

"You'll be in jail while I'm in the hospital."

He shrugged. "I doubt it. Your word against ours. We're football players and everybody likes us. You're the little shit who got A.J. killed. And I think you'll change your mind once you're a bloody mess."

"You didn't even like A.J.," I said. I started to say more but he spit in my face and stepped back.

"We got it all figured," Ray Martel added. He was in Precalculus with me last year and we always got along okay, but now he was looking at me like I'd kicked his dog. "We divided the team into squads. You're good at math—figure out how many squads of six are on a football team."

More laughter. Briggs added, "And we all pledged to pound on you if you don't keep your mouth shut and take the beat-down you deserve for killing A.J. He was my teammate even if we weren't friends, and teammates stick up for each other."

"You tell 'em, Billy."

"Damn right."

"Fuck yeah, I heard he cut the rope on A.J.," said his moron friend Mears. "I heard they were roped together, and A.J. slipped and was hanging there, and Monkey Boy got scared and cut the rope."

I glared at him. "That was from the movie *Touching the Void*, you dumbshit."

Some of the others laughed and Mears told them to shut up, then slapped me across the face, hard. I tasted blood and spat at him, but he moved out of range just in time.

"Real fucking brave."

"So you want to fight me if they untie you, tough guy?"

"You outweigh me by like eighty pounds, and there are six of you."

"Hey, we play to win," Mears said.

"You're still a dumbshit."

That was the truth, but it made them laugh in a mean way. Hitting people was how they solved problems on the football field—and sometimes off it.

A door behind me banged open, filling the garage with light for a second before it was slammed shut again.

"Hey Casey, just in time. We're about to put a beat-down on Monkey Boy."

Briggs said, "What you doing here? You're on the second squad, remember?"

Casey walked over and looked down at me. Then he looked up at Briggs. "I've never been on the second squad in my life."

Nervous laughter. Briggs said, "No, I mean, I came up with the idea, and you didn't raise your hand to volunteer for the first squad. You know you woulda been on it if you did."

"Had to think about it."

"Well hey, since you're here, why don't you take the first punch." Briggs looked around the room. "Remember guys, just one good shot each, for A.J. Then we drop off Monkey Boy at the emergency room."

I was thinking, yeah, if Monkey Boy is still alive. These guys were big and strong and angry enough to kill me.

Casey nodded. "That's a plan," he said. "But here's a better one. All of you get the fuck out of here now, before I put YOU in the emergency room."

Stunned silence. Mears started to say something, and Casey took two steps toward him and looked down right into his eyes. I saw instant fear, and, when Casey's gorilla hands curled into fists, sheer terror.

"You want the first punch?" Casey asked. "You want to try me?"

"No, dude," Mears said, backing away. Casey followed

him so close it was like they were dancing. "We were doing this for A.J.! We were doing this for your best friend!"

That stopped Casey. He looked around the room. "You guys all miss A.J., and you're all pissed off he's gone. So am I. And tell you the truth, I wanted to bounce Jordo around some myself. But first I wanted to make sure."

"Make sure of what?"

"That he was responsible."

"He was there when it happened!" Briggs yelled. "They were climbing partners. That makes him responsible!"

"No, it don't," Casey said. "I talked to the state patrolman who showed up right after it happened. I talked to some other climbers who've been on those rocks. They all said the same thing."

"What?"

"That it was an accident. Jordan didn't have anything to do with A.J. dying."

"Bullshit!" Briggs shouted, and a couple of others repeated it.

Casey stepped toward Briggs and shoved him in the chest. "You calling me a liar?"

"I'm saying you just … you just don't know … "

"I told you I DO know. I talked to people who were THERE. And I know Jordan. He don't lie. And HE was A.J.'s best friend, not me. You think he'd do something to hurt his best friend?"

Silence again. A player by the door opened it and walked out, followed by others. Some looked at Casey;

most just looked at their feet. Briggs and Mears were the only ones left, and they were sort of shuffling, looking at each other, maybe thinking that together they could take Casey.

"Yeah," Casey said, reading their intent. "Let me untie Jordo and we'll have a fair fight. Me and him against you two shitbrains."

He started working on the knot behind my back. They looked at each other, then back at Casey like he was nuts. "You think Monkey Boy can help you in a fight?" Briggs asked with a smirk.

"Well, you guys add up to about four bills together, and so do Jordan and me. Plus, it would be two against two, and Jordo is tougher than he looks. That too complicated for you, Briggs?"

They were pondering that when the knot came loose and I sprang out of the chair and kicked Mears in the balls. He was off guard because he was looking at Casey, behind me, and he fell down and started rolling around and groaning. As I kicked him a second time, in the gut, I saw movement out of the corner of my eye.

The world spun. Briggs had punched me on my cheek. A solid shot, and I would've been zonking z's if he'd hit me a little lower on the jaw. I went down hard, but wasn't out—so I had a front row seat to watch the rest of the action.

Because Casey Ragurski is so big, people sometimes make the mistake of thinking he's slow. I've been watching him play football for years, but even I sometimes forget how quick he can move. In a flash, he took three steps, lowered his right shoulder, then lifted his right arm violently. Briggs' chiseled chin lifted off Casey's forearm like a rocket. The rest of his body followed, and he flew about five feet before he hit the garage wall. He crumpled to the floor like a rag doll, his eyes all spacey for a second before they shut.

Casey looked down at me. "You okay, Jordo?"

"Yeah," I said, but I wasn't sure yet. I knew I'd at least be sore the next day, and my face would be a nice shade of purple. I needed ice and painkillers.

"We make a pretty good tag team," Casey said, looking at the still-groaning Mears. I thought he might've killed Briggs, and maybe he did too, because he went over and checked him.

"Breathing's fine," he said. "Be asleep for a while, though."

I managed to stand up, but I was all shaky. Casey put an arm around my shoulder to steady me. "Take it easy, buddy. I'll give you a ride home."

"Thanks."

"Sorry about going along with this shit for a while."

"Yeah, well, I get it. Glad you reconsidered and saved my ass."

He smiled. "Just like freshman year."

"Yeah, I owe you for two."

"Have Juana set me up with that tall friend of hers," he said, "and we'll call it even."

"Done deal."

He helped me out to his truck. On the way to my house he called some of the other football players on his cell and told them to go take Mears and Briggs to the hospital.

I started to breath easier and, despite the pain and shakes, I felt almost giddy with relief. "Thanks for demonstrating Newton's second law of motion," I said.

"Huh?"

"Force equals mass times acceleration. You're the formula brought to life."

"Oh. Kinda like speed plus size means trouble?"

"Pretty much, yeah."

At my house he asked if he should come in and explain things to my mom and maybe apologize, but I told him no, I could handle the rest. I could tell he was relieved—size and strength don't matter when you're dealing with a pissed-off mom.

TWENTY-ONE

Life is either a daring adventure or nothing.
Security does not exist in nature, nor do the
children of men as a whole experience it.
Avoiding danger is no safer in the long run
than exposure.

—Helen Keller

Senior year was okay after that, even great at times. Mom pestered me for a while after I came home bloody and bruised. I wouldn't tell her who jumped me, though I assured her it was all over and things would be fine. And things were, except for the times I'd think about A.J.

A lot of people were thinking about A.J. His spirit seemed to hang over Mountain View High and the city of Everett. I remembered Zenny talking about Everett's collective bad karma from the Massacre. I don't know about that, but it sure seemed like the town had a collective sad karma about A.J. We all needed his smile and energy, and we were dragging without it.

The football team was the most obvious victim. Even without their best player they had a lot of talent, but they lost close games they could've won if they'd played with more intensity. That's what Casey told me, anyway. They finished 5-5—not bad, but disappointing after going to State the year before and having such high expectations.

Casey had a good year, of course, and made first team All-State and All-American and All-Everything Else. He accepted a football scholarship to the University of Washington, and spent the winter in the weight room and put on fifteen more pounds of muscle. He also grew another inch, making him six-six and two-ninety. Nobody in his right mind messed with Casey, and ever since we'd renewed our friendship, no one messed with me, either. All I had to put up with the rest of the year were some dirty looks from Mears and Briggs. No problem.

．　．　．

A couple of rocks sort of defined the school year.

The first was Juana's idea. The school had been looking for a way to honor A.J., and Juana wrote a column in the first issue of the *Free Sasquatch* proposing a monument. Most people really liked the idea, including Principal Denny.

Juana's monument was a rock she saw at the base of Index Town Walls, a hunk of granite about three feet high and two feet wide and longer at the base. As she described it, the rock tapered to less than one foot wide at the top, and faded to one side. A natural indent in the top was about six inches deep. The idea was that it would fill with water when it rained. Juana said the water would reflect the sky after a storm and look like tears on the broad face when it overflowed. The hollow would also suggest the holy water holders at the entrance of cathedrals.

Some religious traditions are worth emulating, she wrote.

Juana led Casey and me to the rock in late October. It was a small boulder, really. Even Casey could barely lift the thing, but the three of us managed to clumsy it along the trail and into the bed of Casey's truck, though we had to stop a half-dozen times to rest. The effort seemed appropriate somehow, sort of purifying.

We spent hours cleaning and polishing the rock. Then we hired a professional, at school expense, to chisel the simple words: *In memory of Andrew James Stevens, April 11, 1992–July 27, 2009. Loving son, brother, and friend.*

Principal Denny had the idea to place a granite bench across from the rock so people wouldn't have to stand when they visited the monument, and we all liked the idea.

The monument was dedicated at a voluntary assembly on the day before Thanksgiving break, with members of the community invited to attend. There were even more people there than at the memorial service. After a few comments, Principal Denny unveiled the rock. There was a moment of silence for people to pray, or just think about A.J., and then a line formed and people slowly walked by and looked at the rock. A lot of people touched it and left flowers and cards. Everyone seemed to agree that A.J. would've liked it.

. . .

The second rock was a diamond.

Our parents knew that things had cooled for a while with Juana and me, so they were a little surprised last fall when we got back together, hot and heavy. I felt a jolt of happiness every time I saw Juana, and she felt the same when she saw me. We tried to keep our expectations to a minimum, but upon further review, I changed my mind about being a second-story man. I've decided to be a teacher instead. I like math, I'll have summers off for climbing, and I seem to have a knack for conveying information to the folks in my belay classes. It just all makes sense.

Over the holidays, Juana and I talked about getting engaged sometime after we graduated from Mountain View, and married after we graduated from college. We liked the idea of a commitment, and knew her parents would be less freaked out about us sleeping together if she had a ring on her finger. It was a win-win solution.

By March, we'd both been accepted to Western Washington University in Bellingham, which has a good teacher-training program. The plan is that I'll study math, she'll study literature, we'll both study education, and we'll look into sharing an apartment off campus.

Mom cried in a nice way when we told her the plan. She hugged Juana and said she always wanted a daughter, which got Juana crying, and they started talking a mile a minute, mostly about shopping for stuff. I told them I'd give them time to bond, that I'd go over to the gym for a workout before dinner.

Mom told Juana she'd be back in a minute and followed me out to the porch. "Have you two told the Millers yet?" she asked.

"Tomorrow. We flipped a coin to decide which P-Units we'd break it to first. I lost."

Mom laughed. "Well, she's a great young woman, Jordan." She put her hands on my shoulder and looked me in the eyes. "You know what you're doing. You're a man now, so no more advice from me."

"I might need advice sometimes."

"Well, if you ask, okay. Otherwise I'm staying in my own business. Might take me awhile to break the habit, so cut me some slack. Just know that that's my intention."

"We're going to Yosemite after graduation."

That stopped her for a second, and I could see she wanted to weigh in with a negative opinion of that idea. But she caught herself. "Just be very careful."

"Always."

At You So Mighty, Pete hugged me and slapped my back when I told him the plan. "Goddamn, Jordo, I would've told you to see the world first, do some more hairy climbing. But you're marrying a climber and an adventuress! Perfect! Fucking perfect!"

He called Marie. I could hear her shriek, and he handed me the phone. She sounded really excited, and when I told her Juana wasn't there, she was home talking to Mom, Marie said she'd call them and go join the girl talk.

Pete broke out some Havana cigars he'd smuggled across the Canadian border, and we sat around smoking and smiling and coughing for a while before the work-out. We did a little stretching to warm-up, then started climbing routes, starting with 5.5 and moving up. I lost Pete at 5.10.

"Could've climbed that a few years ago," he said. "Ah well, at least I'm aging gracefully."

. . .

In late April, Pete and Marie were married at Bridal Veil Falls out near Index. The bride and everybody else wore hiking gear, since it was a mile up the trail to the falls. The falls are very misty and do resemble a bridal veil, in a way. Masato presided, with vows written by Pete and Marie. She joked that she had to cross out all the cuss words and references to mistresses.

It was a small ceremony, with Marie's two grown

daughters, Mom and Zenny, me and Juana, and about a half-dozen folks from the gym. Afterward, we formed two lines and the couple ran beneath an arch formed by our ice axes. The reception was in the back room of the Mexican restaurant in Sultan, and then Pete and Marie flew to Hawaii for their honeymoon.

A couple of weeks later, Mom had Zenny over for dinner. They'd been seeing each other more now that the cat was out of the bag, and he stayed overnight sometimes. After dessert, she went to her room and returned with a box. She sat down and opened it. A diamond was inside.

"My mother gave this to me, with instructions to pass it down to one of my children who might want it for an engagement ring. You get it by process of elimination." Her eyes were red from trying to hold back the tears. Zenny stood behind her and gently massaged her shoulders while smiling at me.

I'd been saving for a ring. I told Juana it would take awhile, but we'd be formally engaged sometime before the end of the year, maybe at Christmas. Now we could get engaged anytime.

I hugged Mom and told her it was the best present she'd ever given me.

"When do you think you might pop the ol' question, Jordo?" Zenny asked.

"Well, not before graduation. It would be too weird at school."

He nodded. "Probably true."

"Over the summer."

"You going to tell Juana about the ring?"

"No, I want to surprise her. She knows it's coming in the next year or so, and I got her ring size already."

"Great! You can get it mounted, then," Mom said.

The ring was ready the day before graduation. That afternoon I sat on the bench facing A.J.'s monument, thinking about him and all that had happened. I thought about dying young, and life moving by too fast sometimes. I thought about Juana and Mom, and Pete and Zenny. I hadn't really drawn any conclusions from these random thoughts when they suddenly organized themselves and an equation flashed through my head: Life equals Time by Love to the fourth power over Death.

Or: $\text{Life} = \dfrac{\text{Time x Love}^4}{\text{Death}}$

It might sound kind of morbid, but you need Death in the equation. Pete taught me that. Death keeps it real and reminds you that every minute is precious and full of possibilities—holds that you have to reach for.

I wrote down the equation. It wouldn't stand up to any proof, but something about it comforted me. I said goodbye to A.J. and went over to a copy shop, typed out the equation, hit print, cut out the equation and laminated it. Then I put it in my wallet for easy reference.

. . .

At graduation, Casey had the idea to keep a chair empty in the center of the front row, with A.J.'s football jersey and a cap and gown draped over it. It was still a happy day, and we all seemed ready to move on with our lives. Juana and I hugged and kissed when we found each other in the crowd. I was happy, but I didn't expect to levitate. I felt myself going straight up in the air, though, and it took me a second to realize it was Casey, sneaking up behind me and showing affection in his own way.

"Put him down, you behemoth!" Juana yelled.

"Sure thing," Casey said, dropping me. "What's a behemoth?"

"A defensive lineman who doesn't know his own strength," she said.

"Yeah, that's me."

We wished him luck at U-Dub and promised to make the drive down from Bellingham in the fall to watch him play in the Apple Cup against Washington State. Then he picked up Juana, lifting her overhead while she squealed in mock protest. A photographer captured the moment, and the next morning that picture was on the front page of the *Everett Journal-News.*

Juana and I packed that evening, then dropped by a couple of celebrations. Our classmates were planning to party all night, but we had other plans. I dropped Juana off about eleven and was asleep before midnight.

We were up early the next day and drove all the way down to Ashland, Oregon. Juana's idea. Ashland is famous for its Shakespeare Festival, and she insisted that we splurge on a hotel room and watch a production of *Macbeth*. I wasn't too excited at first, but Juana was, and it was sort of contagious—like with Mom with Rainier. I actually liked the show. We took a little drive afterward and saw Mount Shasta glowing in the moonlight. We decided we'd have to climb that gorgeous peak together sometime, even if it was a walk-up.

The next day we slept late and enjoyed the hotel. Juana wouldn't hear of leaving before the noon check-out, so we watched a movie on cable and had breakfast in bed. Felt like we were married already.

We drove Interstate 5 that afternoon to a camp-ground in Sacramento Valley. The highlight of the night was when we were getting in our sleeping bags and I said, in my deepest voice, "Why don't you scooch over here and cuddle with Bubba?" Yeah, I stole her line. She was squealing with laughter, though, so I don't think she minded.

We were at Yosemite the afternoon of our third day. I was driving into the valley when she caught site of El Cap.

"Pull over! Pull over!"

I did, and she bolted out the door. Then she started jumping up and down while looking at the massive face. I got out and jumped with her awhile.

We found a campground near Yosemite Village, set up our tent, and met some friendly climbers at the site next door. We woke to a fine morning, and were both too excited to eat much breakfast. We packed up our gear and headed to the crags.

I had a little extra weight, in a small black box zippered inside my climbing shorts, that I planned to give to Juana at the top. I smiled, thinking about that, and had to remind myself to focus on the route—though it wouldn't be a problem once we got started. Focus is often a function of altitude. And fear.

We'd decided to start off with a route called, appropriately enough, Commitment. A 5.9 with three pitches. We stepped into our harnesses and checked our carabiner gates.

"You lead, Jordan," she said, grabbing the belay device.

"You sure?"

"Yup, you've wanted this even longer than I have."

"Okay," I said, tying a figure eight with the rope.

"Let's climb this one for A.J."

"For A.J." I nodded, and she gave me a kiss for luck.

"On belay?" I asked with a smile.

"Belay on."

Above me, I saw a cloud that seemed to be falling into the cliff, becoming part of it. When the last trace was gone, I looked at the rock before me. A good hold was just above my head, and I reached out.

"Climbing," I said, and started up the wall.

© Sears

About the Author

John Foley is a writer and a teacher in Vancouver, Washington. His first teaching jobs were in Native Alaska villages, which led to his memoir *Tundra Teacher*. *Hoops of Steel*, his first novel, is based in part on his experiences as a basketball player, and *Running With the Wind* draws on his year living on a sailboat in the Puget Sound area. Foley has also worked as a newspaper reporter in the Chicago suburbs and in Alaska.